Invisible Underwear, Bus Stop Mommies
and
Other Things True To Life

by

·Karen Rinehart

PublishAmerica
Baltimore

First printing

ISBN: 1-4137-1190-1
PUBLISHED BY PUBLISHAMERICA, LLLP
www.publishamerica.com
Baltimore

Printed in the United States of America

To my family:

Scott, Morgan and Melanie, who, if you met them, would beg you not to believe everything you read.

Acknowledgements

Inadequate but sincere thanks to everyone who has written to tell me they can relate.

Thanks to my crackerjack editors / spell checkers, namely my mom, Loretta Buffer, and my cousin, Sara Lomasz.

Thanks to Melanie Chitwood, for being my constant friend, encourager and most of all for being able to see it all happening.

A special acknowledgement goes to the Kintyre-Rathlin Bus Stop Mommies. Though we are but one little corner in an entire universe of mommies who linger long after the bus leaves…though some of our kids don't want to be seen with us in public anymore…remember that we are part of something big…something powerful and fundamental. Something that lasts long after our kids stop riding a bus to school.   See you at the corner.

Grateful thanks to every newspaper editor who's believed in the universiality of *True To Life*.

To find out how to get *True To Life* in your newspaper, get Bus Stop Mommies™ gear, or contact Karen, please see www.karenrinehart.net.

A special hello to Anna.

For the love of every child…please learn more about a very special place:
Victory Junction Gang Camp
311 Branson Mill Road
Randleman, NC 27317
1-877-VJG-CAMP
www.victoryjunction.org

Advance praise for *Karen Rinehart* and *"True To Life"*:

"I've seen Karen Rinehart and I know her closely-guarded secret: she looks like that stunning little gal that drank the Sherpa under the table in Indiana Jones, only spunkier. And just so you know, she pulls this off without a particle of pretension or even dignity. She routinely comes out with lines quoted so many times over water coolers that she should get royalties:

"'I stood there with snot shimmering on my shirt, a whiny kid on my hip and another running through the house naked except for the Desitin smeared over every inch of her body.'

"When she took a gift certificate into Victoria's Secret, her husband in tow, you know it's been too long since they've gone on a date when she reports: 'We wandered around the underwear tables. So many choices, so little fabric. There were so many thongs I felt like I was in the sling shot isle of Outdoor World.'

"If Karen's gems could be mined from the page, her readers driveways would be graveled with rubies."

—Ron Wiggins, columnist
Palm Beach Post

"Karen Rinehart is a mother you'll identify with if your family life is also ripe with comedy moving at breakneck speed. She reports live from the eye of the hurricane that is her daily life. She catches every jewel in the daily whirlpool and with expert aim, hollers out a playful, 'Catch!' to the reader. An easy read by a funny, energetic storyteller."

—Suzette Martinez Standring, Vice President
National Society of Newspaper Columnists

"After a day of juggling kids, husband and housework, most mommies collapse into the nearest easy chair. Not Karen Rinehart. She sits down and writes about it. So read this 'First Mommy of Humourous Column Writing.' She'll make your day.

—Wayne Stayskal, editorial cartoonist,
Tribune Media Services

"Karen's columns appear in our 'Sunday Commentary' section. I love them. They always make me smile."

—Azurede McGinn, Letters Editor, Tampa Tribune

"I absolutely love you and have never even met you—I think my husband thinks I'm crazy because I'm constantly reading your stuff to him out loud! I'm sure there are so many mommies out there that feel the same—keep up the great work Karen!!!"

—Anne :)

"I burst out laughing! Thanks for the laughs, Karen!

—Sheila

"Thanks for the great laugh, loved the Victoria's Secret story."

—Suzanne

"Love all your articles—the one about becoming your mother hit home with me. I think we all reach that stage of life."

—Pat Parrish, faithful reader

"I no longer look for the grocery ads first in the Wednesday edition but your column...."

—another mother

"Thanks for the laughs. You remind me of some of my girlfriends and the silly stuff we talk about. I graduated from UAHS in 1980 and saw your note on the website. Keep up the good work."

—Suzanne, Plano, Texas

"*Excellent column*. I was laughing and saw myself in it."

—Suzette, Boston

"I've looked forward to receiving your colunm, but until tonight, I didn't realize just how much! I thought that I would *die,* I laughed so hard! 'Naming the Dog' has *got to be* the funniest joke to come down the pike in a long, long time!

"My mama doesn't have a computer, so I print the jokes and things out and mail them to her about once a month. This one could not wait! Mama had to lay the phone down, she laughed so hard. I think she may have even taken a bathroom break while I was laughing on my end!"

—Tammy, Mississippi

"I have to let you know how popular today's 'True To Life' column is! One of my friends came in to work this morning saying 'You've Got To Read This!! It is just how I feel!!' And she was clutching your article. She really enjoyed it and as she's passing it around the group, I'm hearing a lot of laughter! Of course, I immediately let everyone know that I'm one of the prestigious Bus Stop Mommies!!

"Anyways, feel good that you brought a lot of laughter into Bank of America today!"

—Mindy, Charlotte, NC

"*Thank you!* I always could use another laugh, especially when it is from a fellow mother. I wish you much future success. Bless you! Carry on with you great work to connect with all mothers in the great spirit of humor and friendship."

—Laura , Columbus, Ohio

"OK. I'm laughing, I love your column, I forwarded it to some friends. Keep it coming, I love to laugh with you as you share so eloquently about your 'normal' life.   .

—Jill, Powell, Ohio

"I laughed out loud when I read your article......how true! I hope you don't mind, but I did forward it to a few other friends who have the mid-summer blues trying to escape from the children!"

l
—via e-mai

"Oh my gosh, Karen! Your columns are hysterical!! I was laughing out loud! I never laugh out loud. I'm one of those people who really doesn't even like jokes. Let's put it this way, a joke has to be super clever and funny for me to truly laugh, and not just fake it. Honestly, you are very talented. I thoroughly enjoyed your columns, especially the one about Sr. Maria! What a hoot! I can't wait to have a few more minutes to read the rest."

—Kathy, Williamsburg, VA

"You have a knack for reaching people in a way that makes life seem humorous. It really does help us to go on knowing we are not alone and that things really do have a funny angle. By the way, becoming my mother was never a bad thought but is an aging process that catches some of us by surprise. Thanks for the memories as well as the heads up! My future is looking brighter because of your writings."

—Nancy

"Victoria's Secret apparel——$19.95. Your Victoria 's Secret story—priceless."

—Palmer, Charlotte, NC

"I need more laughter in my life and your descriptions of your family certainly mirror my own in a way that makes me smile."

—Cyndie

"*Huck-yuck!* I was in a totally foul mood most of the day but just decided to sit down and read a few more of your columns. Now I've had some *seriously* good chuckles and can face the rest of the crap this day will bring. Thank you."

—Sarah, Nashville, TN

"I just read a page that featured your 'Bus Stop Mommies' and it brought back memories you would not believe! I am going through déjà vu, as my grandchildren are at this stage in life, and it seems what goes around comes around. Maybe I should say, 'The more things change, the more they stay the same.'

"I would love to forward Bus Stop Mommies on to my children and grandchildren. Besides being hilarious, they are down to earth and right on the mark!"

—Sandy

"You have a talent to make people laugh with all the right words. Thank you."

—Susan

"You have a talent for making ordinary things hilarious!"

—Lizzy

"I just love your pages. I am sure there are a lot of us mommies (old &young) who can relate to your experiences. Keep up the good work. This old world needs a lot more of laughs instead of sorrows."

—Ellie

"Thank you! The realism and laughter made my day!"

—Erica Best

"I just wanted to say 'thanks' for your column. I read it in *The Independent Tribune* every week. In fact, it's the first thing I look for in Wednesday's paper.

"I am a 40 year old, home-schooling mother of six (ages 14, 13, 6 ½, 4, 2 ½, and 8 months), and it totally blesses me to read your column. So many times we take life too seriously, and I am so thankful for the humor-filled way you look at life. You give me a much needed laugh every week and help me put into perspective the 'norm' of everyday life."

—Beth, Concord, NC

"So funny I was almost crying!"

—Sharon

Contents

The Secret of Life

A sentimental favorite of many, this is where it all began: my first column.

The Bus Stop Mommies (aka The Secret of Life)

You can learn a lot about life from standing at the bus stop. In particular I'm talking about my children's school bus stop in my North Carolina neighborhood.

We moved here last February, more than halfway through the academic and school bus year. At our school in Florida, there was no bus system, so every morning and afternoon I took our lives in my hands while I maneuvered the drop off and pick up lines. Long before I had children, I watched the school parking lot scene in the movie, "Mr. Mom", and haughtily concluded no mother in a school parking lot could possibly be that rude.

Then I had children of my own.

When I stand before the judgment throne in Heaven, I'm sure there will be a separate and infinitely long line specifically for Parental Parking Lot Sins. God knows I've witnessed and participated in more than I care to admit. "Hey you moron! Could you drive a little faster around all these little kids?"

"So Karen, I see your husband picked up the kids yesterday."

"Why yes, I was home sick in bed. How did you know it was him?"

"He was in the wrong line…you need to talk to him about that."

HONK HONK HONK "Oh pardon me, was I in the way of your big truck or was it your big ego?"

Then there was umbrella toting Sister Maria manning the lot like Schwartzkopf with his tanks. You knew you had "arrived" when Sister reprimanded you for leaving your car in the pick up lane unattended or nabbed you chatting with the van in the adjoining lane, thereby stalling the forward progress of the pick up line. Parking lots can bring out the worst in me, plus send a horrendous message to little wide-eyed-sponges-for-brains children in the back seat.

That said, you can imagine my great joy of leaving behind parking lot rage and racked up minivan mileage. Except on the first day. Then I was just plain nervous watching my child climb aboard that big orange thing on wheels with a stranger for a driver and no seat belts in sight.

Anyhow, last February, the weather was cold and wet so none of my new neighbors were outside to accost, um, I mean introduce myself to. I was desperate to feel like I belonged in this tight knit 'hood and especially anxious to meet the other moms. For a reason that escapes me now (big surprise) my husband walked our daughter up to the bus stop that first anxious morning.

I pressed my nose on the cold glass of the front door and after wiping off the fog and grime, could see them gathered around the bus stop at the top of my street...yes! They're there! All my future friends and fellow vessels of homework and hormone wisdom! Oh how I longed to belong. You see, I've learned that life's ebbs and flows and passages of time have less to do with great mystical omnipotent powers, but rather with how long your children have been riding the bus.

The bus stop: A true suburban bevy of sleepy eyed, mumbling, bed-headed creatures. And the children aren't always so perky either. They are still trying to get their mothers out of bed. Our driver has won "Bus Driver of the Month" every month since school opened this year. Translated: she's never late. As a matter of fact, she's typically early. She even smiles in the morning and has the heat on for the kids during the winter. She's still smiling in the afternoon...a far better person than me, she gets to skip that long line in Heaven; I'm certain of it.

The Bus Stop Mommies agree with me. We tend to agree on a lot of things as we discuss all of life's crucial topics – who has the best prices on milk, what time the mail comes, who needs to bag their grass clippings, fourth grade writing tests, which teachers were meant to become prison wardens, which laundry stain fighter is the best, how to remove moldy shower caulk and anything related to the male species.

The Bus Stop Mommies always know where and when the next Tupperware, book club and birthday party will occur. We are never more than a house away from a borrowed egg, wallpaper scraper or glass of Chardonnay. Within their ranks I have found women who share my faith, doctor and distaste for ironing. All things wise and wonderful...they are mouthed at the Bus Stop. The Secret of Life...learned at the Bus Stop. The Be All and End All...you guessed it, The Bus Stop.

So the next time you need a walking buddy, a third opinion on the color of yellow you just finished painting your kitchen, or just some mommy venting time, head to the bus stop. Call one of the gals and have her meet you there early.

Therein lies your answer.

My Idol

I needed to pick up my daughter from Alma's house and I was nervous. Alma is my idol. I'd been worshipping her at the bus stop for months, but since we'd always swapped kids at the corner, had yet to step into her house. According to Bus Stop Mommy lore, Alma designed and decorated her house herself, right down to sewing the curtains, reupholstering the furniture and hand dipping the candles.

She's the only mom at the bus stop who had a Valentine's gift for the bus driver. It was a gold Godiva box wrapped in a real fabric ribbon, tied in a large red bow. Tucked under the bow was a hand-addressed envelope that didn't have "Your postage helps feed a hungry child." scratched off first.

That was the morning I offered to put her youngest child on the bus while Alma drove her other daughter to school early. In her impeccably clean car. Wearing ironed, matching clothes and makeup.

There I stood in my reindeer pajamas and parka, holding the bus driver's gift, when the other moms circled around, coffee cups trembling.

"Hey Rinehart, what's the big idea making the rest of us look bad? I thought we had a pact."

"It's not mine!" I yelped. "It's Alma's. Her daughter's too shy to hand it to the driver so I agreed to do it."

"Well then, who's got a pen? Let's add our names to it."

Alma's the one who always has her roots touched up on time. She wears lipstick to the bus stop when the rest of us wear yesterday's mascara. On our cheeks. I've never seen her nail polish chipped. She knows all the good scoop from school and has the common sense and logic to decipher the facts from the folly.

She's simultaneously finishing her Masters degree, running the Girl Scout cookie campaign and church charities. She delivers her kids on time to soccer practice, clarinet and horseback riding lessons, then cooks them meals with more than two colors. All this on four or five hours of sleep each night. I know, because I'll get e-mail from her time-stamped, "12:39a.m." with the next one marked, "5:42a.m." And they're coherent.

I felt the overwhelming need to clean my house before I walked over to hers…but I snapped out of it, dug my lipstick out of a crevice in the minivan and headed over.

The smell of dinner wafted through the air. We relaxed in her gorgeous living room where Alma actually rested her feet on the white ottoman. "Coffee?" I gazed across the foyer. There was a plant with three dead leaves. The dining room table looked as if it hadn't seen the light of day since last Easter. The candles were leaning and every stair had a pile on it. The whines of bickering girls echoed over the banister. "I'd love some."

And I love that woman.

Figuring Out Friendship

What are the marks of a true friend? They seem to change as we age and move through life. Or do they? These thoughts have rumbled around my skull for a while now; usually when I should be concentrating on other things, like measuring the salt in the cookie dough or sorting the one hidden red item from the pile of whites.

No small wonder this week I was buying bakery cookies and telling my son that if those kids were really his friends they wouldn't make fun of his pink socks.

But then again, he's in eighth grade and those Middle Schoolers are a weird bunch. At that stage in life, there are numerous untold hidden agendas, cliques, social rules and dress code violations that can make deciphering who your true friends are a real trick.

Younger kids are pretty straightforward. Toddlers get along with each other as long as they don't touch or look at what the other one has. Friendship in toddlerhood consists of the slogan, "It's Mine so back off and we'll all get along."

Once they hit school age, kids start adding rules or codes for determining what makes someone their friend. It moves slightly beyond the simplicity of, "Hey Boogerhead, what part of 'It's Mine' don't you understand?" to "I like you because…"

Through exhaustive research, (peeking in the neighbor kid's backpack) I located concrete examples of the complexity of friendships in elementary school life. When asked to describe what made a particular classmate "super duper," local third graders wrote the following (spelling and grammar unedited):

"Since your favorite game is blackjack I would say it's a good game."

"I think you are a lot like my dorky brother because you like Yogio."

"You're a super duper awesome friend and your funny you like the same things as me like Mr. Pibb and pizza."

"You looked cute on your fast day of school."

"You are very silly and funny you also have a lot of friends because you are so funny!!"

"I really like the way you play and talk. I knew you would be a good friend

27

at the begineing of the year. I am in scouts like you. That's all I half to say about you see you later by."

"One of my favorite pop is mr. Pibb to."

"We have a lot in comen, like my favrit coler is blue, we like hamsters, both like pizza."

"I like blue so do you. Do you play sports? You're a good friend to use. My favorite subject is math but yours is science. I like playing with you every day."

"I really liked the poster that you made."

"Your nice friend in class. Your very fast to."

"I like legos too."

"You are fun energetic, and a really good tager when we play tag. You and I both like pizza. You are a really good A+ student. You look so cute on your first day of school. With your little lunch box and all. You're a really nice person."

"It's like a disese, every boy in this class likes blue."

So there you have it. Food, soda, talking, fun and games. And the occasional diseased boy. Doesn't sound too far off from the ties that bind the Bus Stop Mommies.

Maybe time doesn't change the marks of friendship that much after all.

Sometimes it takes me a while to figure things out...

Life Lessons: The Fever

So, how's the barfing at your house? What about the sore throat, muscle aches, fevers and headaches?

If you've been spared any of the above this season, you're luckier than anyone I've talked to recently. Either that or it's just lurking somewhere outside your door, building up momentum for the big hit.

The flu monster knocked down our door yesterday afternoon. Technically, it hit the remote control on the minivan power sliding side door and climbed inside.

"Mom, my head is killing me. I need ibuprofen. And my chest hurts. And my throat feels worse than it did this morning. Can you turn the air conditioning on full blast back here? I'm burning up."

Having my son home sick as a teenager paints a vastly different picture than having him home sick as a young child.

As a baby, he had perpetual ear infections. I don't know who screamed more and slept less—him or me. For his first birthday he got a set of ear tubes and we finally learned what more than two hours of sleep at a stretch felt like. He was like a whole new child. We were happy. Rested.

Then he hit the elementary school age years. The doctors kept calling them upper respiratory infections. The allergist called it a sinus infection. The kid ate antibiotics like candy and became quite proficient at coughing himself into barfing fits. I became proficient in functioning on very little sleep, changing sheets at midnight and writing school excuse notes.

Finally, five pediatricians later, Dr. Mary took one listen to our son, threw him on a nebulizer and introduced us to the wide wonderful world of asthma. The poor child had been misdiagnosed and mistreated for years. Now he could be treated properly and get back to living an active little boy life.

Missing school in the elementary years meant a minor backlog of class work and maybe a missed indoor soccer game, but nothing earth shattering. Now with high school fast approaching, grades "counting" and baseball tryouts on the line; getting "sick" gets a little more complicated.

Some things about being sick, however, don't change. When the toddler ailments hit, I learned very quickly that children's pain reliever/fever-reducers weren't necessarily a good thing. When I let the fever ride itself out, my little red-cheeked cherub cuddled on the couch with his blankie, sippie cup and me—the greatest living being in the universe. According to the feverish mind, I outranked the dog, Batman and Barney combined.

When I gave my son acetaminophen, his fever broke. For the next three hours, my "sick" little cherub danced on the tables, ran matchbox cars up the walls and measured my worth according to how many times in a row I read the Golden Book edition of Bambi without skipping pages.

A decade later, I relearned this: Fever? Good. Acetaminophen? Bad. Give the kid a couple little tablets and in no time he transforms from a couch ridden, shivering, mumbling lump under six blankets to a couch ridden, chipper, chatty, TV remote clicking lump under two blankets. And yes, he's hungry.

So this morning, when my big boy woke up once again spiking 101, I poured more Gatorade, tucked the blanket under his chin, enjoyed a rare snuggle and hid the acetaminophen. It's been a very quiet day.

Productive Day Guilt

"I don't want to keep you. I know you've got a lot to do today," said my friend phoning from Sarasota. I wanted to scream, DON'T HANG UP! Keep talking! Nothing is more important than this conversation right now.

Well, to tell you the truth, I think I left the lid up on the washer and the suspense was kinda killing me but wait – what is so earth shattering important in my gloriously domestic day that I can't take time to talk to a dear friend? The dust isn't going anywhere and the dirty Fruit of the Looms will keep piling up until I'm good and ready for them.

Unfortunately, I wasted years of potential domestic bliss worrying about being productive. My husband came home every two weeks with a paycheck that proved he'd been productive every day. I stood there with snot shimmering on my shirt, a whiny kid on my hip and another running through the house naked except for the Desitin smeared over every inch of her body.

Blame it on the feminist movement of the 60's and 70's. Blame it on my college degree. Whatever the reasons, I felt that as a stay-at-home mother, I had to prove myself. I needed to produce tangible evidence of my productivity during "all that free time" at home. I was stupid.

A productive mother is one who, at the end of the day, typically knows her children's names by the third try. She might even remember her own name and address.

By the end of the day, the children of a productive mother will have eaten something, even if it were defrosted ten minutes before mealtime. They most likely will have used a toothbrush, on their teeth, at least once. They're clean enough that even the dog will lick them. Their bathrooms are cleaner than those found at a rest area.

Every member of the household has enough underwear or diapers for one more day. Then again, even the most productive mother occasionally turns off her mind-reading capabilities and is informed by a resident teenager at 6 a.m. that his underwear drawer is empty. This is why baby powder was invented.

When our kids were still babies, my friend Beth called and shared with complete ease: "Sarah was sick yesterday and the only thing that made her happy was to be held and rocked. So that's what we did all day." I remember wishing I could sit and rock my baby boy without worrying about what wasn't getting done.

31

Yesterday, I brought my teenage boy home from the hospital following surgery. I pumped him full of pain medicine and got him settled on the couch. I pulled over the rocking chair, sat down and watched him sleep for hours.

It was a very productive day.

A colleague wrote and asked, "Hey Karen! It can't really be that bad, can it?" She's single, without children.

It's The Day...

It's the day you spend one hour vacuuming the house and three hours trying to dislodge a pink Barbie comb out of the vacuum cleaner engine.

It's the day you vacuum and shampoo the minivan only to realize it's your turn to haul the entire red Gatorade drinking Oreo munching soccer team tomorrow.

It's the one day out of the month your husband is available for lunch only to realize it's the one day you committed to baby sit a friend's child so she can go to a doctor's appointment.

It's the day you got a sitter for the baby, switched preschool carpool days, set the alarm thirty minutes early to put on makeup and iron a shirt in order to get to school for the class party, only to find out your kid told you the wrong day.

It's the day you rush out the door to meet the bus on time, stub you toe and spill your Starbucks on your shirt only to have your kid say, "Why didn't you bring the dog?"

It's the day you remember to bring the dog to the bus stop but he sees a cat and pulls you into the half-shut door which hits your brow bone so hard you see stars, but you stumble to the bus stop anyway only to have the kid say, "Why are you late?"

It's the day you spend the morning in bed trying not to puke then the rest of the day in the bathroom puking but manage to put dinner on the table only to have the kids say, "Gross, I hate this!"

It's the day you stay up until 2 a.m. finishing the Halloween costume your child would die if they didn't have, only to have your kid declare at the light of day, "Never mind Mom, I'm just gonna wear last year's costume."

It's the day you spend hours dusting every last knick-knack, window blind and piece of molding in your family room only to have someone light a fire without checking to see if the damper was open.

It's the day you mop the white linoleum kitchen floor only to have half the soccer team run in off the rain-soaked field for a snack with their cleats still on.

It's the day you do every load of laundry but the 'reds' only to have your kid tell you at 10 p.m. that he needs his red shirt for gym class tomorrow.

It's the day you splurge for a sitter so you can go shopping and have lunch with your girlfriend only to have your kid wake up with a high fever and the runs.

It's the day you cave into your maternal conscience and put clean sheets on those stupid bunk beds only to throw out your back and be forced to cancel the hair appointment that's made your life worth living for the last two weeks.

It's the day you're cemented to the couch with the bad back and heating pad, wondering if you'll be incapacitated through the rest of the fall planting season, only to have your daughter bring you a "Get Well" drawing, a root beer and a kiss.

It's the day that anything that could possibly hit the domestic fan and fly in your face does; only you realize it's going to be okay.

But What Do I Know?

My mother is one of those people gifted with the ability to give a smart answer to a silly or invasive question as soon as it's asked. I am not. Five minutes or a day later, I'll think of what I wish I'd said. So don't be too critical of these answers. I only had a few weeks to think about them.

Answering The Questions

Funny thing about people—they tend to want answers to questions…including the ones I shared with you several columns back. Just when I thought enough weeks passed, I was reminded of my unfinished business. "Mom, I still think you need to write a column with all the answers to those questions."

"Son, I have a word count limit."

"So?"

"So, it would take too long to answer all those questions and besides, I doubt anyone remembers that column anyway."

The next day I was at the newspaper office when the editor, Dale Cline, shouted above the cubicles, "Hey Karen! Just how fast were you going?"

Fine, okay, all right already.

I'll take 'Questions I Ask Myself' for 500, Alex.

Kmart or Wal-mart? Whoever has Sutter Home on sale for under ten bucks a bottle.

Where's the dog? Outside barking at cats and eating grass.

Did I already put detergent in here? Who knows but a little more won't hurt.

Have I brushed my teeth yet? Who knows, but a little more won't hurt.

Where are my keys? Right where I left them five minutes ago.

HGTV or TLC? Depends when Martha is on.

What is that smell? Anything that came off my children's feet.

Am I normal? Define normal.

Did I put out the recycling bin? Yes, because it's overflowing and I need the room for this week's wine bottles.

Am I scarring my children for life? Of course. It's in the How to Be A Successful Mother manual.

I'll take 'Questions Presented To Me In Public' for a thousand, Alex.
Does this match? No and it's a horrid color for your skin type.
Are you Greek? Yes. I am Crisis, Goddess of Maternal Bliss.
Paper or Plastic? Paper. The kids need new book covers.
Do you work? No I sit and eat bon-bons all day.
How do you want that sliced? Opaque thin. I feel like I'm getting more ham that way.
Air freshener with that wash? Only if it's free.
Can I see your ID? If you promise not to laugh at the picture.
Are all those kids yours? Why, you want to rent one?
Have you always been that short? No, I used to be five feet five inches but it was boring being of average height so I had myself shrunk down to five feet even.

OK Alex, I'll struggle with 'Questions My Kids Ask Me' for five bucks.
Where's the toilet paper? Same place it was yesterday when you asked me.
Where's the dog? I thought you had him.
What's that smell? Put your shoes back on.
Where's my book? Check the bathroom.
How do you spell idiot? Look it up.
Will you tell her to flush? Flush.
Will you tell him to put the seat down? I swear if I sit down on the toilet with the seat left up one more time you will be sooo sorry young man.
Have you seen my shoes? Look under the couch.
When is dad coming home? Good question.
Did I really come out of your stomach? No, you were a blue light special.
Do I hafta? Yes.
Have you seen my hamster? Ask the dog.
Who ate the last Fig Newton? Not me. Smell my breath.
How did you know that? I'm a mom.
Why are you clenching your teeth? Hoo heeph me phwum sshcweeming.
Are you going to the bathroom? No. I'm reading.
Can I come in? No. I'm reading.
Can I have something to eat? Sure, if you can find anything.
Will you get mad if I tell you? Define mad.
Do we have any lighter fluid? Yes, right next to the ammo and peanut

butter on the pantry shelf.

Moving on to 'Burning Questions From Moms of Younger Children' (priceless):

Do all their teeth really come in? Not before the first ones start falling out and the braces go on. Then, when the crying fits, diarrhea and drooling have ended, you'll pay to have the rest pulled.

Is my kid normal? Do you really want me to answer that?

Am I normal? Of course dear, of course. Now blow your nose, take your little blue pill and go home.

Is there life after diaper rash? Yes. It's called teething.

How much did those braces cost you? Sorry, can't talk. Have to rush to my third job.

Why are you laughing? To keep from crying.

And finally, the Daily Double for a million dollars Alex, 'Questions My Husband Asks Me'

Have you seen my (fill in the blank)? On your dresser.

Where is (fill in the blank)? Under the kitchen sink.

Who is (fill in the blank)? Your sister's mother-in-law.

What is (fill in the blank)? Your son's science project. Don't touch it.

Why do we (fill in the blank)? Because I said so.

What time (fill in the blank)? 7 p.m. and don't be late.

How do you (fill in the blank)? Push the knob in then turn.

Where do we keep the (fill in the blank)? Refrigerator, second shelf down, back left corner behind the horseradish.

And of course,

Have you seen the remote? I thought you duct taped it to your forearm.

So there you have it. I hope my answers satisfied your long burning curiosity – pardon me? I forgot one? You want me to tell you how fast I was going? Do I hafta?

I heard from a lot of moms who have mornings like this. Some of them though, just let the dog eat the crayon.

Bad Mom, Bad.

This week has done nothing to boost to my Maternal Goddess Psyche. I feel like I've fallen to the bottom of the list of bottomed out moms. And it's only Monday morning.

For the third time I poked at the motionless blob under the blanket. "Time to get up, I mean it! I am not driving you to school if you miss the bus." Nowhere in my Mommy Manual does it say I have to be compassionate before my first cup of coffee.

What the blob under the blanket said: "I AM getting out of bed Mawmm (whine moan) and I NEED that money for the field trip!"

What I heard the blob say: "If I don't bring in that money today I will be the laughing stock of the entire class. You're such a loser; I can't believe you'd risk ruining your own child's life by being the last mother to deliver the field trip money."

"Field Trip? Which one?" I swear this kid spent more time on field trips than in her bed or school combined. We had to give up meat this week to pay for them all. $15 here, $8.50 there, and, as the blob enlightened me, another $2 today (bargain!) for a trip to the Glenn Center. I haven't a clue what or where the Glenn Center is, but the detail-less permission form was written assuming I knew.

I bet every other mother filled out that form the day they got it. I bet each of those mothers not only knew what and where a Glenn Center is, but could drive there in their sleep and locate every county approved fire exit throughout the building. If it's even a building. I figure it can't be anything too fancy since it's only a two-dollar trip.

I shuffled to the kitchen and stared at the piles. I have a highly organized system of household piles, which, no matter what it looks like to the untrained eye, allows me to locate any piece of paper within 2.7 seconds. Unless of course, someone, who shall remain nameless, but has the initials h.u.s.b.a.n.d. messes with my piles…which he had the wherewithal to do over the weekend…conveniently prior to hopping the first flight to Jersey Monday morning.

I simply didn't have it in me to start digging. I swiped a piece of notebook paper out of somebody's backpack and wrestled the black crayon away from the dog.

"This note gives my daughter blah blah permission to attend the field trip on blah blah to blah blah place. I solemnly swear not to hold the school system responsible should anything unpleasant occur on this trip. Then again, bear in mind I might feel otherwise (1) Once I am caffeinated and (2) If the unpleasantry is a direct result of my strong requests to keep the school bus bully far away from my child having gone unheeded. Enclosed is the money (that I was going to use to supply a year's worth of rice to a child in Uganda) for the trip.

Sincerely and legally yours, Karen Rinehart"

I sealed the note and money in an envelope and handed it to my child as we walked out the door. "Look, I hand wrote the permission note because I have no idea where the original one is. If they don't like it, have them send another one home tonight and I promise I won't lose it. Better yet, just blame it on your dad. He isn't here."

I Know Your Mother

There's only so much you can hide from your friends. And your neighbors, your husband, your husband's colleagues, your husband's colleague's neighbor's husband, your kids, your kids' teachers and the librarian downtown. It's inevitable. Don't even try to fake it.

One day someone you know is going to be your child's substitute teacher and your cover will be blown for good.

My friend Lilly called this morning on a matter totally unrelated to my true self being exposed in public but somehow that came up, too.

"Did your son tell you I was his substitute teacher last week?"

"Oh yes, and he really liked you. He's my sweet child, that boy."

"Oh I know. I asked him what it's like to live with you...if you made things as wild at home as you do other places. Like book club. He said, 'Oh well yeah, kinda. She can get real loud when she gets mad.'"

She was laughing so hard at this point I'm not sure she heard me nervously chuckle something about my Italian temper, heh heh. Silently, I was thinking how lucky my sweet little boy was to currently be home quite sick and miserable, thus preventing me from really acting Italian. Just wait till he feels better.

Not that I can blame him for being so honest. Or blame Lilly for asking. I've been a substitute teacher at my children's school before. There's nothing quite so powerful as the knowledge that you know someone's mother.

The first and second graders look at you with awe and wonderment in their eyes. How could this be? You know my mother? It's like telling them you personally know Santa and that the Tooth Fairy is your next-door neighbor. You are magic in their eyes and they spend the rest of the school day submissively following your every directive. They share their cookie with you at lunch.

Third graders are still pretty cute and trusting and don't make a lot of trouble.

Fourth and fifth graders start thinking for themselves. "Hey Johnny. Sit at your own desk and keep your hands to yourself. I know your mother."

"Oh yeah? How? What's her name? Where do I live?"

"Tennis. Lorraine. In Sister Maria's office if you don't take your seat this instant."

Johnny is quite polite and obedient not only for the rest of the day but every other day you sub the rest of the year. The other kids take their cue from Johnny. They are not yet stupid at this age.

Middle Schoolers fall into two categories. Those who offer to take names when you leave the room and those whose names are taken. The name takers are the ones who had kids like Johnny in their class for the last two years and they missed the stupid boat. They also have parents who don't let them talk trash or talk back.

The kids who give you trouble are the one who either had stupid marshmallows in their cereal that morning, weren't paying attention when Johnny got silenced, or talk back to their parents. But even these kids respond favorably to, "I know your mother."

I teach an 8th grade Confirmation class on Sunday nights. I used to have several rude, disruptive students. Used to. I finally held up my cell phone and the class roster and said, "I know your mothers."

Whatayouknow? You're Just A Mom!

Today I'd like to share with you a short chapter I've memorized from The Mommy Manual. It's entitled, 'Whatayouknow? You're Just A Mom!'

This is the attitude children adopt as they approach the teenage years. Unfortunately, it can hit girls many years earlier, while some boys tend to fall into it later. As you know, the mommy manual is grossly under-detailed and we're left to either flounder around or seek answers from wiser, more experienced Bus Stop Mommies.

The chapter does include a few general examples to help realize your child has entered the 'Whatayouknow?' phase.

* You say, "It's cold outside; wear long sleeves and your coat."
  They leave in a T-shirt.
* You say, "That kid down the street is no good." They invite him to
  spend the night.
* You remind them to stick with their assigned group on the field
  trip. They wander off with the no-good kid from down the street.
* You make a brown bag lunch. They leave it on the curb at the bus
  stop, pretend it was an accident and charge against their account
  at school.
* You say, "Don't forget your glasses." They do. On purpose.
* You suggest the brown shoes would look much better with their
  dress pants. They wear their yard mowing tennis shoes. You don't
  see it until you're walking into the church/restaurant/school inter-
  view.
* You say, "Have an apple. It's almost dinner time." They grab the
  bag of chips and hide in the bathroom.

The chapter has a sidebar on suffering from S.O.S. Syndrome: Sudden Onset of Stupidity. You go to bed one night thinking maybe you haven't scarred your children for life after all, and then wake up in the morning to learn you know nothing at all.

This syndrome can strike at any time, but reaches epidemic proportions during the teenage years. The best and brightest parents are not immune. It's tricky in that it's not immediately contagious—it can strike you first, but not affect your spouse until next month or next year. Apparently, the only cure is the passage of time.

The scariest thing about SOS Syndrome, is that the sweetest, most obedient of children will fall prey to its side effects. Little children, who once believed you when told there wasn't a boogieman under the bed, will now scoff at your every word. If you tell them rain is wet or fire is hot, they'll set out to prove you wrong.

I'd hoped a vaccine would be invented before I entered the high-risk age group. It's painful to imagine my 'little boy' turning on me. My hopes were dashed when the mother of my son's best friend called to tell me she's been diagnosed with S.O.S.

Inconceivable! I think so highly of that kid I'd let him eat out of my secret emergency chocolate stash and now he's gone off and turned on his good mother!

Fear struck my very core—if the mother of that adorable, obedient, mild mannered boy could be hit with S.O.S., so could I.

Send chocolate. I'm not ready.

From Birth Onward

Birth of a Teenager

Four days and counting. That's all I have left of life without an official teenager in my house. I mean, one I actually gave birth to. Between baby sitters, friends, neighbors and the occasional 'who was that kid?' this place always has some form of teenage life lurking near my refrigerator. But now I'm talking about my own son. My (sniff), first born. My baby – waaaaaaa (and that's not him crying now).

Where has the time gone? I swear it was just yesterday that I was enduring the tenth day of being overdue in the sweltering Louisiana summer heat. My mother had flown to town, two weeks earlier thank you very much, to help me through the birth of my first child. Picture this – my husband, my mom, a dog, cat and waddling station wagon on legs all crammed into a one-bedroom apartment. More than one of the couples in our Lamaze class, and I am not making this up, had skull and cross-bone decals emblazoned on the rear windows of their pickup trucks. We had two dollars to our names and two friends in the whole city and they were off on their honeymoon. Traitors!

On my second wedding anniversary, the three of us (we left the cat and dog at home) spent a romantic evening in some dark auditorium at a Southern Living Cooking Show. The overdue overactive child in my womb tried his best to get out and sample the food that night but to no avail. The perky lady on stage spewed on about garnishes while I tried not to spew, period. The lady sitting next to me a little less than tactfully got up and found another seat across the room. She was sure I was Sigourney Weaver and the alien was about to be born right there before dessert was ever fixed.

The next few days after my anniversary were a blur of long hours camped by the pool in futile search of relief from the heat and boredom. My husband kept a close eye on me to ensure I didn't drown as a result of my unstable girth or even more unstable mental state. I was so miserable the man agreed to paint my toenails, which of course I hadn't seen in months. My mother, God bless her, kept me fed and as sane as humanly possible.

Finally, at the proverbial Hollywood time of 3 in the morning, my water broke. At least I was pretty sure that's what happened. I mean, all the doctors, nurses, Lamaze instructors and books tell you to go to the hospital when your water breaks—this indicates the big point of no return. The problem is, no one ever really tells you how to distinguish between this momentous occasion and the commonplace occasion of just laughing too hard while coincidentally being nine months pregnant.

I figured at this far along, a trip to the hospital would not be wasted if I garnered some Graham crackers and apple juice; I was starving. Mercifully, my doctor was already at the hospital finishing a delivery and soon appeared to give me the stay or go verdict. After two false labors and overnight stays in the hospital already, I was a little gun shy of hearing his news. "Pleeeeze don't make me go home this time, Daryl! I beg you! Please tell me this time I'm leaving here with a baby in my arms."

"I promise you you're not leaving here without a baby. Of course it could be a while…" Famous last words. And from a man who's never given birth.

Over eighteen hours later, Dr. Daryl was again at my side (well, in a manner of speaking; he was actually at my toes) but this time without a smile on his face. Fine with me, I sure as hell wasn't smiling at this point despite all the drugs they'd pumped into me. "Karen, the baby is in distress. I think it's time we consider the other option." Without hesitation, I lifted my sweaty head off the pillow, glared at him from between my knees and hissed, "Open the zipper and take it out!" Fearing my head would start spinning on its axis, Daryl sprinted away in search of the surgical team. My husband, of course, was relieved to be relieved of his bedside duties and was sent down the hall to hang out with my mother.

Finally, at 10:06 p.m., little Morgan was lifted into the world and screamed heartily much to the relief of his mother. Thirteen years later, again to my relief, he's given up the screaming. He's replaced it with mumbling and all sorts of other prerequisite teenage behavior. I know now, on the eve of the official teenage years, that we are entering the Great Unknown, just as we did the eve of his birth thirteen years ago. There will be good times (A/B honor roll, public acknowledgment of a parental figure), bad times (eye rolling, talking back, skyrocketing food bills, discovering girls) and everything in-between. Through it all may God give me the grace to say now and in the future what I said thirteen years minus four days ago—

"I'll keep him."

My Blonde Haired Daughter

My son has brown hair (and eyes) like me, but my daughter's hair is a shimmery shade of dark blond with faint hues of amber. Up until age 7, her hair was pure, glistening golden blonde. Although she acts like me (lucky girl) she looks nothing like me, which at times is downright depressing. Just yesterday, I stared at Melanie reclined in the orthodontist's chair and realized she'd pass for the doctor's daughter before she'd pass for mine.

With her vivid blue eyes, she's garnered comments from total strangers since her earliest days. I'd take the kids to the grocery store (after charitably giving my personal shopper the day off) and get all sorts of unsolicited comments about my children. Fortunately, they were mostly compliments, though there was the occasional, "Hey lady, your kid is about to dive head first out of the buggy!"

A typical and oft repeated encounter would go like this:

Me: Walking through grocery store, kids in cart, desperately trying to remember what was on the grocery list I painstakingly wrote in chronological order coordinating with the grocery store isles but left on my kitchen counter.

Stranger: "Oooooooh! What a beautiful child!"

Me: "Thank you. Do you know what was on my grocery list?"

Stranger: "Her eyes are SO blue!" Looks at my eyes.

Me: "Yes they are. Thank you."

Stranger: "And that lovely golden hair! (Sigh) I've never seen eyes that BLUE before!" Looks at my hair, down to my chest, back up to my eyes. (Squints).

Me: Wishing I knew how to wiggle my nose and disappear, "Um, thank y..."

Stranger: "Hey Herman, come look at the eyes on this baby. You've never seen them so blue!"

Me: Realizing my bladder is full and I can't remember if I've even gone to the bathroom yet today, "Thank you so much. Oh, hello Herman."

Stranger: "She's so beautiful... she must look like her father."

This scenario ranks only second on my list of 'Depressing and Deflating

Conversations' to the one I had with my husband just after said daughter was born. I had to be knocked out for the C-section (a relief to my husband who was on the verge of passing out) but woke up momentarily in the recovery room to see my now not so woozy husband narrating the videotape, Life After Birth, starring Karen Rinehart. Perhaps something deep within the thick walls of his brainiac carcass told him I couldn't leap off the gurney and kill him, making it safe for him to film me in such a horrific, painful, bad hair state.

Hours later, I woke and asked, "So, what does she look like?" Without the slightest hesitation, my dear husband answered, "Ah Honey, it's great! She looks exactly like Morgan when he was born." Three years earlier when Morgan was born, he looked exactly like his father.

So let me get this straight: I endured endless months of nausea, night sweats, indigestion, waddling, hemorrhoids, poking, prodding, needles, cellulite, stretch marks, tacky maternity fashions, excruciating pain, thinning hair and scars that resemble the Hymilaen mountain range only to have both kids get yanked out and look just like their father.

Remember him? The one who almost passed out as he sat and held my hand behind the tall blue 'can't see a thing if you tried' draping? Our children look just like him.

He's taking them grocery shopping from now on.

Babymania at the Bus Stop

It started as a typical morning at the Bus Stop. Most of us had waved goodbye to our middle-schoolers and were now waiting for that orange chariot from heaven to arrive and take away the elementary school kids. The Bus Stop Pets, Chelsea, Blondie, Ginger and Hank, were pouncing all over each other; thoroughly tangling their leashes and coating themselves with wet grass, mud and slobber.

The Bus Stop Mommies were talking about all our friends and neighbors who recently announced they're pregnant. The predicted, standard retorts rang out:

"Better her than me!"

"How many does this make?" and "How old is she??"

But this morning, some remained silent throughout the heckling.

Then they calmly and quietly spoke.

"I'll be 46 this year and we're talking about having another child."

Then another, "I'll be 40 next year and haven't ruled it out either." While a few of us were pulling our slippered feet out of our mouths she added, "The thing that has brought me the most fulfillment in my life is my children. Nothing else comes close."

"EWWW!" I squealed in delight. "Have babies, you guys! I'll help you!" The other BSM's doubled over in laughter. "Gee Karen, exactly how would you fit into this process? Is there something we don't know about?"

Okay, so I was thinking of throwing baby showers and babysitting, but in my usual graceless style my mouth opened before my brain functioned.

Anyhow, we started discussing the modern attitude towards (or should I say against) having more than 2.3 children, let alone having them after some mystical age. Why do other people care how many kids we have or how old we are when we have them? It's not like I'd ask anyone else to change their diapers, pack their lunches, pull the Lego out of their mouth or keep them from playing in the toilet. Seems to me it's between a wife, her husband and God.

"When I told a good friend of mine, who's a nurse at the hospital, that I wanted to have another child, she got hysterical and yelled, 'We have special rockers here for people like you! Come in and hold all the babies you want.

Then you'll get over it.'"

My middle-aged friend continued, "I don't want to just hold a baby, I want my own baby. Those rocking chairs won't help me. This isn't some phase I need to 'get over'."

I could totally relate to my friend's sentiments. I've wanted a baby for most of the last 10 years. I still haven't gotten 'over it'. If one more person tells me the only reason I 'think' I want another child is because I physically can't have one, I might have to call my cousin Guido.

As a matter of fact, sitting in some hospital rocking chair with a baby would make me want one even more. Oh sure, there are moments I chide myself for wanting to start babydom all over again...like when I put on something labeled 'Dry Clean Only' or sleep past six on a Saturday. But then there are moments when all it takes is a whiff from an opened bottle of Baby Magic Shampoo and I'm in tears.

"But Karen," someone noted, "you whine and stress about the children you already have." Sure I do. I also whine and stress about my husband, driving a minivan and the price of chocolate covered espresso beans...but do you think that means I don't want them or love them any less?

Toddlerhood Revisited

Just when I thought my potty training days were over, my best friend's children came to stay at my house. Overnight. Without their parents in attendance.

I was so excited to have a toddler in the house again (somebody remind me I said this when I take them to the pool later today). I climbed up on my husband's car, which was no small feat since he just waxed it, and retrieved our old training potty from the garage shelf. It's one of the few pieces of toddler paraphernalia we saved. You'd be amazed how much time you save on a road trip when you take that puppy along in the minivan. "Mawm, I gotta go!" every thirty minutes no longer causes migraines.

I hosed out the Little Tykes receptacle, dried it to a high shine and brought it inside. I lovingly placed it on the kitchen counter and said to my husband, "Look!" For some reason his face did not light with the same glee as mine. In my mind a slide show of the three hundred pictures we took of our toddler children on said potty was clicking away. Scott's mind saw the potty and conjured up visions of the Microsoft Money page that reflected the annual diaper budget converted to the annual orthodontia budget, which will eventually convert to the annual tuition budget…he wasn't smiling.

No matter, Tyler, my resident Toddler, would be excited that Aunt Karen had her very own mini potty for him to use. Never mind the fact that his mother warned me they were in the midst of a power struggle in the formerly successful potty training process. The boy was at Major General Rinehart's house now. Things would be different for me. After all, this was the same child whose mother swore he never stopped talking but played quietly for hours on end at my house.

"Tyler, come with me!" I held the potty in front of me much like the Priest holds the book of Gospel readings for all to respect and anticipate, as we paraded back to my kids' bathroom. "How's this Tyler? Do you want the potty in here?" Tyler seemed skeptical. He gave me the three-year-old version of You're Wasting My Time Lady look, but wasn't quite ready to be outright disobedient. "I don't like this bathroom."

"You don't? OK, let's go see Aunt Karen's bathroom."

The Potty Parade proceeded down the hall, through my bedroom and into my bathroom. I placed the potty, with a great flourish, in front of the tub. "I present to thee, Prince Tyler, thy potty."

"I like this bathroom, Aunt Karen." Bingo! "OK Ty, let's go potty before dinner," I said as I pulled down his training pants and plopped him on the little blue commode. "I don't want to go."

"Sure you do."

"No, I don't wanna go."

"Come on Tyler, you're a big boy. Go pee pee in the potty."

"I can't."

"Yes you can."

"I can't."

"Does daddy go pee pee in the potty?"

"No."

"Yes he does. Go pee pee."

"I can't."

"Tyler, you need to aim that thing down, not up."

"Huh?"

I pointed to the object of his manhandling, "You need to aim down into the bowl, not up, or you'll pee in your face. You don't want to pee in your face, do you?"

"Um, no." He aimed down. Whew, we were making progre—

"Aunt Karen I can't go. My dad flies an airplane. I want a drink of water. Why does the ceiling do that? My mom has that. I'm hungry. Why is this your bathroom? What's that?"

The boy won. He was going to babble away the night and burst a bladder before he'd give me the satisfaction of putting something in that pot. Besides, I could smell the chicken potpies on the verge of burning from here. It was time to pack away my Superaunt pride and admit defeat.

En route to the kitchen I heard a flush and then the sound of hand washing from behind the hall bathroom door. Out came my teenage son. At least I did something right back in my children's toddler days. Again the slide show of my kids in their potty training days came to light: Little tow headed two-year-olds holding Golden Books strategically on their laps; the time my daughter covered herself from head to toe in Desitin in potty preparation; sitting for hours until they fell asleep with bowl marks on their bums; quietly slipping under the restaurant table to go poop; peeing through the wrought iron railing of the front porch as passing cars slowed to take pictures…

On second thought, I'll let his mother deal with it.

Maternal Revenge Phenomena: The Phone

I hate the phone. I really do. Let me communicate by e-mail, fax, the written letter, smoke signals or Morse code, I don't care. Knock on my front door or jot me a note in the dust on my furniture, just don't call me.

I wasn't always this way. My dad recently gave me the light blue princess phone I used in high school. The earpiece is worn smooth from my endless hours of chatting. Several of the tiny holes are actually missing.

I can still hear my mother screaming up the stairs, "For the love of God you just got home from spending two days at her house—what could you possibly still have left to talk about? I've got work for you to do. Get off that phone and get down here this minute!"

As hard as we try, we in some way, shape or form manage to become our mothers—or at least adopt Universal Motherdom Lines (not to be confused with martyrdom, but it's similar). You know the ones, you open your mouth and this alien being slips in and makes you say something that you swore you'd never ever say when you grew up and had kids.

What makes it worse is that somewhere in a seniors' aquacise class in Ft. Myers, Florida, your own mother knows. I swear they just know when their wish for revenge has been granted.

Recently, my 13 year-old son spent a long lazy summer day at his friend's house. His bicycle tires had barely made contact with our garage floor when his friend, who lives around the corner, called him. "Who are you talking to?" I mouthed (I make it my business to know). "Carlos." This time I used my real voice, "Carlos? You mean Carlos as in you just spent all day at his house Carlos?" He nodded.

"For the love of God you just spent all day at his house what else could you two possib—oh crap!"

"Hang on Carlos. Mom? Crap what? Mom, are you OK? Mom, isn't it dangerous to put your head in the oven?" They talked until Morgan saw food on the table. "Yeah man, gotta eat." Half a cow and wheat field later, my son was done with dinner. Time to, you guessed it, call Carlos again.

Fortunately my daughter, who just turned ten, is not yet interested in the telephone. As a matter of fact, she has a genuine phobia of both dialing a phone (what if I get the wrong number? What if a live person actually answers it?), and answering a phone without knowing who's on the other end. I've been encouraging her to make calls and answer with confidence...to get over her dislike of the phone...to call her little girlfriends and oh wait.

Did I just say what I think I said? Someone please remind me three years from now when the cordless is growing out of her ear behind a locked bedroom door that it's all my fault. Eventually, mothers' wishes do come true. But don't just take it from me. Ask my mom. She's the one laughing hysterically in the middle of a Ft. Myers swimming pool.

Who knows where or how M.R.P. will strike next...

Maternal Revenge Phenomena: The Daughter's Room

Let's see, it's been a while since we covered Maternal Revenge Phenomena and The Telephone. Naturally, the time was ripe for a particular retired grandmother in Ft. Myers, Florida to take a break from her aquasize class and cast revenge in my direction.

This time, she's getting back at me for maintaining the room of a princess pig throughout the majority of my childhood. For all those times I whined, "But I DID clean it!" To which she would retort, "And just shoving stuff under your bed does not constitute cleaning!"

Some say pack rat. I say sentimental. How many mothers my age can open a box in the attic and share fond childhood memories with their own children? Just recently my children were captivated by my Wacky Pack Card collection and guppy badges from swim lessons.

It's a miracle I have mementos left to show them. On several occasions, I'd come home from school and notice something askew in my room. Oh no! While I was out, mom had been cleaning out.

If I was lucky, mom didn't time her excavations with trash day, and I was able to salvage a few treasures for posterity. When it appeared I'd spend the remainder of my childhood bent over trashcans in retrieval mode, my brothers started calling me Theresa Trash and Grace Garbage.

One item, I recall fondly, must have been thrown out and retrieved at least three times before I didn't miss it anymore. It was this 12-inch high white plastic chrysanthemum, cemented in a pink fuzzy flocked flowerpot. There were a couple fake green leaves at the base of the white stem and a smiley face glued to the flower head. I can still see that hideous thing sitting in its place of honor on my windowsill.

To this day, I have no idea why I owned it or how it met its final fate, but alas, I have my memories.

I'm sure mom threw out a bunch of stuff I never missed. I only hope I have the same luck with my daughter.

The impending arrival of the carpet cleaner this morning forced me to clear a four-foot swath in her room. That's all, just the entryway. It's senseless to pay to clean the rest of it since it's covered with an area rug, which in turn is constantly covered with all sorts of little girl goo.

Like the unfinished homework assignment from two years ago. Or the oozing Root Beer Barrel Dum-Dum sucker stuck to a birthday goody bag under the bed. Let's not overlook the ever-present "I'm not eating in my room, Mom!" candy wrappers, empty juice boxes, petrified cracker crumbs and ground-in gum wads.

Some items aren't as scary, and in my merciful moments, don't get considered for the trash heap. These include plastic horse accessories, underwear, hair clips, Barbie shoes, human shoes, socks, books, sparkly pencils, crinkled photos and my $15 pair of tweezers she swore she'd never seen. Of course, none of the socks and shoes, Barbie's or hers, have a match; but not to worry. I'll find them the next go around.

As I stowed away her valentines from the last two years, it hit me. That poor girl has become me. I have become my mother. Will the madness never end?

I can only hold out hope that the dog doesn't take after either one of us.

Tear Ductitis

After one traffic jam, near bloodshed over who got the good spot in the parking lot and two elevator rides, I blew into the doctor's office with a miraculous minute to spare. I waited 39 minutes before they took me back.

After repeating my symptoms, social security number and mother's maiden name for the receptionist, lab tech, nurse, nurse's assistant and janitor, the doctor finally arrived.

"So, Karen, what seems to be the problem?" Have you ever noticed that doctors, even ones younger than you or ones that you've never met, can call you by your first name, but you have to call them Dr. So and So?

"Well, Doctor So and So, if you read the chart you'd see why I'm here."

"Pardon me? Your voice is rather hoarse, have you been talking a lot lately? You know, you really shouldn't strain your vocal chords that way. Open your mouth and say 'Ahh!'"

"I'm not here for my throat."

"Then why are you here?"

"Your waiting room always has the latest issue of People magazine. Besides, I think something's wrong with my tear ducts."

Grabbing his penlight he asked, "Are they clogged?"

"Just the opposite; they seem to be overactive."

"Uh huh, and how long has this been going on?"

"Ten and a half years. But it's gotten noticeably worse in the past several months."

"I see. Say, Karen, How old is your youngest child?"

"Ten and a half."

"That would make her in fifth grade, right?"

"Right"

"And she's probably been talking a lot about going to middle school soon. Right?"

"Right."

The doctor sat on the stool and wheeled over, my paper gown stirring in

61

the breeze. "We're not getting any younger you know. When would you say your tear ducts have been particularly uncontrollable?"

"Television commercials, for one."

"Any ones specifically?"

"Hallmark. Especially the ones they ran during the holidays."

"What about promos for TLC's A Baby Story and Maternity Ward? Do those spots activate your ducts beyond control?"

"Yes, doctor! Yes, they do!"

"Uh huh", scribble scribble. "And what about sappy music videos on CMT? Especially that new Brad Paisley one where the father waves as his daughter moves out on her own and the son walks off in his military uniform?"

"That was the worst! I tried to hold it together, but it caused the most painful tightness in my throat, the tears seeped out and before I knew it I was holding my breath and…"

"It's all right, I know. Now, what about church hymns? Slow tunes on the radio? Attendance at class plays, spelling bees and honor roll assemblies?"

"Doctor, it's like you can read my mind. Please help me! It's embarrassing in public. I'm getting desperate here! You've obviously seen this condition before. Tell me. What causes it? Is it fatal? How much time do I have?"

"Relax Karen; it's not fatal. Though there are times it'll hurt so bad you'll think you're dying. Other times it'll hurt so much you'll want to kill someone else. There will also be times of complete joy and pride that will activate the symptoms too. The more you try to control it, the more it hurts. So, just live it. I'll have the nurse get you some samples of waterproof mascara and pocket size tissue packets. You'll be fine."

"OK doctor, if you say so. Thanks. But one more thing. What's it called?"

"Tear Ductitis. It's Latin for, The Youngest Gets Older."

School

School Bullies, Some Things Never Change

The front page of today's newspaper carried an excellent article on bullying in schools. The middle school in a neighboring town has enacted a cutting edge, courageous, anti-bullying program. As soon as I finish this column, I'm heading out the door to find that school and grovel at the principal's feet. Then I'm going to my kids' schools to beg their principals to enact the same program.

Bullying… are the flashbacks hitting you too? I'm standing on the sidewalk outside my first grade classroom. I'm wearing a smashing long, kelly green dress emblazoned with neon pink lions (compliments of my mother and Simplicity # 1222). I was sporting a Liza Minelliesque pixie hairdo (courtesy of my brother who cut off one of my long pigtails that summer) and a mouth full of baby teeth.

Although I didn't notice, I must have stood a head lower than all my classmates. Why else would they pass by me gawking and yelling, "Hey! Look at the Shrimp!" Or come up to me and ask, with genuine research tone sincerity, "Why are you so short?" I'm sorry to say, thirty years later, I still get asked that question. (I wish I could say, "I was born this way; but why are you so fat?") Maybe the experts who developed the anti-bullying program for teenagers can create one for adults.

Here I was, at the ripe old age of six; yet I didn't know I was 'short'. It took my very kind classmates to enlighten me. Even my three older brothers, Curly, Larry and Moe, never brought up the size issue. Called me Grace Garbage for digging stuff out of our trash cans? Yes. Teased me about my size? No.

Flash forward to 2002, when it took a small gang of girls in my daughter's fifth grade class to enlighten her to the fact that she wears braces and glasses. Frankly, our entire family was aghast to learn this! How did we miss such obvious facts all the while living off macaroni and cheese to pay for such entities?

It's amazing how suddenly my daughter started 'forgetting' her glasses after these budding bullies informed her she wore them. Just as quickly, my bright, dramatic daughter with the infectious laugh stopped smiling. After all, that would show her braces and how embarrassing it must be to discover you're the last one to know what's in your own mouth!

This past summer, my 20th high school reunion came and went. I'm certain no one missed my skinny butt on that float in the 4th of July parade. Let's be honest. The only reason I wanted to go back was to say Na Na Na Na Boo Boo in the faces of all the jerks who snubbed me because I wasn't a cheerleader or a blonde, didn't have blue eyes, a rich daddy or long legs.

Oh sure I was smart, artistic, never wore braces and had the latest fashions (argyle socks and kilts complete with giant diaper pin)...but it didn't matter. That just kept me from being shoved in a locker or ending up out in the chain link pen with all the 'Burnouts'. I was smart enough to know that if the smoking didn't kill me, my father would when he found out what I was doing.

Frankly, it would have been a great waste of time and money had I traveled to the reunion. What I really need to attend, if they ever start having them, is an elementary school reunion and a middle school reunion.

Between my hometown paper and my mother's continuing connections, I know I'd show up with a better marriage, better kids, and far smaller butt than most of those former bullies. I'd take my daughter with me too. She has a great brain, blonde hair, blue eyes and long legs. She has zero interest in cheerleading but can confidently guide a four-legged thousand-pound beast through a Dressage ring; then accept her ribbons with grace, humility and oh yes, a smile.

Braces and all.

Stories continue to run on the wires, in the news and health journals on the dangers of heavy backpacks. Rolling backpacks remain banned in our schools. How about yours?

The Dreaded Backpack

This morning at the bus stop, Amy was stuffing snacks into her daughter's backpack – which was as big as she was but weighed about twice as much as this pretty little fourth grader.

"Olivia, you already have your gymnastics snack in here, you don't need this banana too." Mom dropped in the pack o' crackers, zipped the pocket and booted her daughter towards the corner.

Alma and I eyed each other knowingly after witnessing the all too common Bus Stop Mommy ritual, Stuff the Backpack With Last Minute Almost Forgotten Items. "At least she didn't pull out a hermetically sealed package of smashed peanut butter crackers."

"Eww, yeah, that would've been bad."

I mean, what a waste of a perfectly good snack! If they were broken Cheezits or Cornflakes you could at least toss them with some butter and recycle them into the Universal Crunchy Topping used to disguise vegetables. But peanut butter sandwich cracker crumbs? I suppose you could mix in some colored sprinkles and tell the kids it's new a gourmet ice cream sundae topping. I hate to throw them away, they're still sealed in the bag you know. Perfectly edible. Cost good money. Starving kids in India and all that....

Another thing I hate is discovering PE clothes in the deep dark depths of my kids' backpacks. Dirty, damp, two-week old PE clothes. My son has, over the last couple years of middle school life, become more thoughtful in the care of his gym clothes. Instead of leaving them in his backpack, he pulls them out and plunks them on the kitchen table.

He then announces in my general vicinity that they're there…somewhat akin to being presented with the Crown Jewels. One day when he does that I'm going to drop to my knees, bow up and down before him and wail, "I'm not worthy! I'm not worthy!"

Broken pencil stubs, ballpoint pen carcasses and 5-month-old homework assignments are other popular items found lurking in backpack crevices. Fine. But then there's the single dirty sock (belonging to no one in this family), paperbacks from last year's classroom teacher, unidentifiable sticky goo that won't wash off my fingers without mineral spirits, Barbie clothes, golf tees, used dental floss, formerly edible particles now in artifact form, pencil shavings and dog treats.

I surveyed the Bus Stop Mommies this afternoon to see what odd things they've found in their kids' back packs.

"One time after he'd been swimming at soccer camp, Hamilton came home with the wrong shorts and underwear. I could understand the shorts…but the underwear?"

"At the end of one summer we found a lunch leftover from the last day of school. We threw out the whole thing—backpack and all."

"So far I haven't found anything alive but there's still time; it's only August."

"I swear one day last week I saw my son's backpack move but I wasn't about to unzip the thing to find out why."

Thankfully I've never seen Morgan's backpack move, but I've seen him unable to move after carrying one. The picture of him frozen in pain on the school sidewalk is locked in my mind—my little 2nd grader was in a neck brace and on muscle relaxants for a week.

His backpack is no lighter now that he's in 8th grade, nor is the zippered load my 5th grader hauls on a daily basis.

I learned backpacks on wheels were outlawed right after I purchased a new one and stocked it with supplies.

The Bus Stop Mommies and I can only speculate that whoever made this rule worried about the new carpet wearing or the corners of walls getting scuffed. There's a rumor about boys from last year swinging wheeled backpacks around by the handle. Like they couldn't use a regular backpack as a whirling weapon too?

Maybe schools can outlaw backpacks altogether. I'd have less moldy PE clothes in my kitchen…not to mention the task of figuring what to do with those crushed crackers.

School projects. Enough said.

The Living Museum

Perhaps in our paper recently you've seen the pictures of local elementary school children presenting a 'Living Museum'. If you're new to the area, you probably asked yourself or a neighbor what it was and the price of admission. Wonder no longer, here's how it works:

From a teacher-approved list, the children choose (fight over), research, (scan the web) to learn about a famous person. Then, after 6 weeks of preparation (nothing like having a major project hanging over your head during spring break), the children 'become' their person. They dress in costume, gather props (at 7:30 that morning), and assume their post in the museum (school library). When the other children visit the museum, they hand the famous character a ticket, which causes said character to come to life and talk about themselves for two minutes in mostly soft, speedy voices.

The children in my daughter's class were given a list of famous North Carolinians from which to choose their biographical subject. You know, people like Aunt Bee, James W. Cannon, James Taylor, Opie and those two brothers with the flying contraption (although Ohioans are ready to start another civil war over that one). After no less than three newsletters and worksheets for the project, my daughter came home and announced she'd chosen to be O'Henry. "Oh Honey, that's great! I like that candy bar."

"Maawm! He wrote a huge collection of short stories, including, *Gift of The Magi.* Duhhhh!" I was going to ask, "Isn't that the story of Epiphany in the Bible?" but didn't want to see her eyes roll out of her head again.

After dropping her backpack of bricks on the floor, she proceeded to inform her obviously stupid mother that O'Henry's real name was William Sidney Porter and that he created the pen name after his prison guard, Orrien Henry. Turns out ol' what's-his-face had a passion for embezzlement and fleeing from the strong arm of the law…plus his children and dying wife. Not only did the law catch up with Mr. Porter but his philandering lifestyle and overindulgence of whiskey did as well, killing him at the age of 48.

Wow, this was one stellar North Carolinian! I wanted to ask my daughter why she chose such a loser, but she seemed so sure of her choice that I bit my tongue (for the 40th time that day). Why did I care whom she chose for this project as long as she was enthused and did a good job?

Because she didn't choose me! My little feelings were hurt and my fragile ego crushed. For six years, every school paper and art project somehow revolved around me: "Here Mom, I made this for you." "Mom, will you come on our field trip paleeeeze?" "For show and tell today I brought my mom." Had the magical mommy spell been broken? Was I being replaced by a famous felon and drunk? Was she trying to tell me something?

I'd like to think that Melanie knew it just wouldn't challenge her enough to choose me for the role. I mean, she is me already—same mannerisms, facial expressions, hand gestures, sense of humor, divine fashion sense, and irresistible charm. Tell me, where is the academic challenge in that? Furthermore, how hard would it be to pick five props? Broom, checkbook, dishrag, mismatched garden gloves, laundry detergent, receipts, toilet brush, minivan keys, cinnamon gum wrappers, pooper scooper, chips of old picked at nail polish, dog hair covered clothing and an empty box of Chicken Helper…yup, way too easy.

Now actually putting into words what she'd say I'm famous for is challenging. But who am I to run from a challenge? After all, I've given birth and lived to tell about it. I have straight teeth without the benefit of braces. I'm hands-down the most frugal shopper on this side of the Mississippi. I laugh out loud. Real loud. Okay, sometimes I laugh so hard I snort.

Hold on a second the phone is ringing. "Hello? Yes, this is the famous North Carolinian Karen Rinehart. Oh? I see. No need to apologize. Yes, I know it wasn't the candy bar guy. Thanks for calling."

That was Melanie's teacher. It seems the printers left my name off the students' list of famous North Carolinians. She felt real bad about the mistake and apologized profusely. Now I can believe that the Mommy Magic between my daughter and me hasn't disappeared after all.

The Day Off of School...Midweek

The dreaded day-off of school in the middle of the week. It's upon me and taking on its familiar feel.

"Mom, don't forget my project is due in two days."

"Have you started it?"

"No. Can I go play at Sally's?"

"Mom, Bill's mom is taking him to the park. Alison's mom is taking them to Charleston for the day. Fred is golfing with his dad. What are we doing today?"

"We're going to change the sheets on the beds."

A day off of school in the middle of the week in the middle of the school year is kind of like an entire summer vacation crammed into 12 hours. Except it's cold outside, so that rules out dumping them at the pool all day. It's also rainy season, so at least 70 percent of your plans better be indoors.

The expectations run high on the part of the kids. My intentions run high all the days leading up to the day off. I have grand plans—sleeping in, fixing a hot breakfast that doesn't materialize when you pour hot water into it, picnicking and playing in the big park across town, a movie, bowling, visiting the horses in China Grove, lunch with daddy at his office downtown – you get the idea.

Instead it went something like this: Wake up with a jolt thinking we've all overslept and the kids are late for school. Realize it's their day off and snuggle back into my pillow. Crack open one eye and see gray skies outside the window. Mentally scramble to change the day's plans from outdoor to indoor.

Hear children calling dibs on the comics and remote control. Stick head under pillow. Realize children are quiet. Too quiet.

Catapult out of bed and into the family room. See children mesmerized by cartoons. Make coffee. Check e-mail and be reminded of phone calls I need to make. Listen to kid crunching and slurping cereal behind me at kitchen table. Out of the corner of my eye see daughter starting school project on the kitchen floor with utility knife, permanent marker and $8 foam core board, without waiting for help. Look at the clock. It's 8:43 a.m.

Make mental list, prioritizing things to get done today. I'll feel more re-laxed about taking the kids out to play if we do a quick once over of the house first. You know, wipe the sticky goo off the kitchen counters, rinse toothpaste globs out of the sink and put away the clean laundry from last week.

"Mom, the hot water won't turn off in the bathroom sink!" Add to list, Trip to Lowes / Replace Faucet's Washers.

"Mom, I ruined this foam core board for my project! I'm so stupid! My life is over!" Add to list, Trip To Craft Store.

"Mom! I'm riding my bike over to Eric's to take him the notebook he left here." Kid walks out the door. Notebook remains on kitchen table. Add to list, Take Notebook to Eric.

"Mom! We're out of white bread and I hate this Branola stuff." Add to list, Buy Bread.

"Mom, I'm back! I wrecked my bike and I'm bleeding. Did anybody call? What's for lunch?"

It's 9:17 a.m.

Add to list, Pick Up Sedatives At Pharmacy.

"Holidays" and
Other Eventful Events

I still can't believe I did actual, certifiable research for this one. Happy Mother's Day...no matter what the calendar says.

Mother's Day

Well, tomorrow is Mother's day and you know what that means. Some doofus louse of a male who totally forgot to send a card to his mother or take the kids out shopping for his wife is going to curse under his breath and mumble, "I don't know what the big stink is all about. It's just another holiday invented by Hallmark to make money, grumble grumble". Well guess what buddy, you're wrong. It's as official a holiday as the 4th of July and darn near as sacred if you ask me.

According to my intense research, Mother's day has been celebrated under various forms and names since the days of Greek Goddesses (such as my personal favorite, Crisis, Goddess of Domesticity). In 1872, Mother's Day was first suggested in the United States by Julia Ward Howe, who wrote the words to the Battle hymn of the Republic, as a day dedicated to peace. Ms. Howe would hold annual Mother's Day meetings in Boston, Massachusetts. The article doesn't state what was discussed at these meetings but if a little peace and quiet were on the agenda, I'd have been there, veggie tray in hand.

In 1907, Ana Jarvis of Philadelphia campaigned to establish a national Mother's Day. She garnered support from ministers, businessmen, politicians and of course petticoat clad women everywhere. Finally, in 1914, President Woodrow Wilson proclaimed Mother's Day as a national holiday, to be held each year on the second Sunday of May.

How incredibly appropriate that the first American supporter of Mother's Day focused on a day dedicated to peace! I can still see my own mother, year after year, answering our sincere, eager question, "Mom, what do you want for Mother's Day?" And year after year she gave the same answer in the same desperate, exasperated fashion, "All I want is for you kids to get along for once. Just ONE day!" (Add whimpering here.) I hated hearing that – not her whimpering; we got used to that – the "get along" part. I had three older brothers; you think I really had a say in how much we got along? Besides, I couldn't very well walk into G.C. Murphy and ask what aisle the sibling peace serum was in and then pray it cost less than my life savings of $3.17. Couldn't she just want a toaster or slippers like the rest of the moms on the block?

Now that I have children, I can relate to my mother's wishes. My children, whom I love with all my heart and soul, have some annoying habits that drive me to drink faster than their basic bickering. Therefore, when they asked what I wanted this year, my kids heard the following:

For just one day…
* I do not want to hear you Slurp—not soup, milk, saliva or the dog's face.
* Do not eat cereal within forty feet of me—the smell reminds me of first trimester nausea and the noises put chills up my spine.
* Do not whine or otherwise emit high-pitched noises from your Being.
* Do not insult me by trying to lie your way out of trouble, unless salespeople call; then you may tell them I died.
* Do not talk to me while I'm on the phone—this includes, but is not limited to: hand motions, sign language, facial expressions and notes scribbled on paper airplanes.
* Do not, and I really mean this, hover behind me as I type on the computer or read my e-mail.
* Please, if at all humanly possible, refrain from mumbling when you speak.
* Kindly wait 24 hours before making skid marks on the freshly mopped kitchen floor.
* Blow your nose without me telling you to and remember, we are not rationing tissues, be generous.
* Separate your dirty underwear from the inside of your dirty pants before you place them lovingly in your hamper.
* Hang up the wet bath towel (you used once) instead of tossing it in the hamper on top of other clean clothes.
* Let me have sole possession of the remote control.
* Do not pick your nose in public.
* Bring me breakfast in bed. It is not necessary to fan me and feed me grapes but I would like first dibs on the comics. Additionally, it would be helpful if you waited until I set down my coffee cup before you invite the

dog to jump on my bed.

* Knock before you walk into my bathroom.
* And finally, dear wonderful children of mine, just this once, just for one day, promise me you'll never outgrow hugging me.

Now go play outside.

I wrote this a few months before the orthodontist informed me this was simply the end of round three (one and two were head gear and upper pallet expanders). As you read this we are in the middle of round four, lower appliance purgatory. This is running simultaneously with my son's turn in the wide wonderful world of orthodontia.

Thank God for Mac and Cheese.

Daughter Gets Braces Off

I asked her, "How much longer?"

She answered, "10 days, 7 and a half hours and 3 minutes. Oh yeah ba-bee! Oh yeah-ah!"

My daughter is getting her braces off soon. It has been a long, painful journey, these past two years. And at times I recall my daughter taking ibuprofen for pain too.

Originally I promised my daughter a candy party to celebrate the end of the Upper Orthodontia Era. The idea was to invite her friends over and indulge in all the previously forbidden foods – hard candy, bubble gum, Doritos, popcorn, nuts, caramel, taffy and Juju Bees. Did I say candy?

Then we learned the magical date we've been living for the past 24 months, the day 'they come off'. Two days before Halloween. Right there in the middle of the ortho's office she began chanting, "There is a God. There is a God." I yelled, "SCORE! I don't have to host the candy party – the neighbors are doing it for me!"

"There is a, Godwhataya mean I don't get a party?"

"Sweetie," I reasoned, "It's silly to have a candy party when you're going trick or treating two days later." She seemed to buy it but I felt a little guilty. What could I do to mark this momentous long awaited occasion? What else? Write a song.

The Twelve Months of Braces

(Even though there were 24, sung to the tune of The 12 Days of Christmas)

On the First month of braces, orthodontia gave to me, A Payment Plan the size of a tree.

On the Second month of braces, orthodontia gave to me, Two Orthodontists and A Payment Plan the size of a tree.

On the Third month of braces, orthodontia gave to me, Three Styles of Head Gear, Two Orthodontists and A Payment Plan the size of a tree.

On the Fourth month of braces, orthodontia gave to me, Four Appliance Turn Keys, Three Styles of Head Gear, Two Orthodontists and A Payment plan the Size of a tree.

On the Fifth month of braces, orthodontia gave to me, Five Plaster Impressions… Four Appliance Turn Keys, Three Styles of Head Gear, Two Orthodontists and a Payment Plan the size of a tree.

On the Sixth month of braces, orthodontia gave to me, Six Tooth Extractions, Five Plaster Impressions… Four Appliance Turn Keys, Three Styles of Head Gear, Two Orthodontists and A Payment Plan the size of a tree.

On the Seventh Day of braces, orthodontia gave to me, Seven Sets of X-rays, Six Tooth Extractions, Five Plaster Impressions… Four Appliance Turn Keys, Three Styles of Head Gear, Two Orthodontists and a Payment Plan the size of a tree.

On the Eighth month of braces, orthodontia gave to me, Eight Returned Claim Forms, Seven Sets of X-rays, Six Tooth Extractions, Five Plaster Impressions… Four Appliance Turn Keys, Three Styles of Head Gear, Two Orthodontists and a Payment Plan the size of a tree.

On the Ninth month of braces, orthodontia gave to me, Nine Brackets Breaking, Eight Returned Claim Forms, Seven Sets of X-rays, Six Tooth Extractions, Five Plaster Impressions… Four Appliance Turn Keys, Three Styles of Head Gear, Two Orthodontists and a Payment Plan the size of a tree.

On the Tenth month of braces, orthodontia gave to me, Ten Bands A – Popping, Nine Brackets Breaking, Eight Returned Claim Forms, Seven Sets of X-rays, Six Tooth Extractions, Five Plaster Impressions… Four Appliance Turn Keys, Three Styles of Head Gear, Two Orthodontists and a Payment Plan the size of a tree.

On the Eleventh month of braces, orthodontia gave to me, Eleven Late Appointments, Ten Bands A – Popping, Nine Brackets Breaking, Eight Returned Claim Forms, Seven Sets of X-rays, Six Tooth Extractions, Five Plaster Impressions… Four Appliance Turn Keys, Three Styles of Head Gear, Two Orthodontists and a Payment Plan the size of a tree.

On the Twelfth month of braces, orthodontia gave to me, Twelve Ounces of Fluoride, Eleven Late Appointments, Ten Bands A – Popping, Nine Brackets Breaking, Eight Returned Claim Forms, Seven Sets of X-rays, Six Tooth Extractions, Five Plaster Impressions... Four Appliance Turn Keys, Three Styles of Head Gear, Two Orthodontists and A Payment plan the Size of a tree.

I Miss the Norelco

It's not the Christmas season until Santa rides down the snow covered hill on the Norelco razor.

At least that's how it was when I was growing up. Now I'm afraid my kids think it's Christmas in August. It seems like that's when the stores start hawking the tinsel and cashmere.

Back in September, I went to Lowes for gardening supplies only to find the shelves stripped bare with strange little inventory tags taped about. They can't be serious. This can't be happening. Then I spotted it. The first gleam of glitter reflecting off the halogen light fixtures. A lone ornament sat anxiously waiting for hundreds of its comrades to join it.

My husband went to Lowes this weekend for irrigation supplies. They were all put away to make more room for Christmas decorations. Great. The rotating sprinkler heads replaced by rotating reindeer heads.

Something's just plain wrong when you can't buy a swimsuit in June because space had to be cleared for the leather coats. Pretty soon we'll be buying Easter candy at Halloween and Halloween candy in March. The Easter bunny will need therapy. The Leprechauns will have to trade in their little green spring jackets for winter parkas.

What would happen if housewives ran homes on a retailer's schedule?

"Hey Mom, I need a poster board tomorrow morning for my school project."

"I'm sorry dear; the Mother's Union Bylaws won't allow me to purchase poster board after the official start of the school year. You'll have to wait until next summer... or go see Tommy's mommy. She's a line crosser."

"Hello Mrs. Rinehart, would you like to buy popcorn to support my Cub Scout Troop?"

"No can do Adam. My microwave only accepts popcorn packets April, May and June."

"Hi honey, I'm home. What a rough day at the office. What's for dinner?"

"Sorry, dinner was at 2:30 this afternoon. The kids missed it too. Let's go out."

Last year at this time, I was a little behind in getting the holiday boxes down from the attic. (OK, I'm slack this year, too.) When my kids painted fireplaces matches watercolor pink and purple and stuck them in a fruitcake, I decided it was time to buy candles for the Advent wreath.

I found a store that still had Christmas decorations in stock but not the candles. I asked a clerk for help. "Advent candles? For the love of the Irish, Lady, this is the first week of December!"

"I know, but Advent just started yesterday. I still have three and a half weeks of candle burning left. Will you be getting any more?"

"I doubt it. We've got to make room for the 4th of July crafts. Could you use red, white and blue candles?"

I was seeing the better part of red, white and blue when I drove past a shopping center last October and saw the workmen putting up the Christmas wreaths and bows. I almost ran my car into one of the freshly garlanded light poles. Purely by accident, mind you.

I pulled in next to the Chinese Restaurant with the Menorah in the window. "Hey Mr. Workman! Aren't you guys putting those up a little early this year?"

"Are you kidding me?" he shouted back. "We're behind schedule. We were supposed to have these up last month but were swamped with working on the St. Patrick's Day parade."

Maybe those matchsticks aren't so bad after all.

What We Did Over Spring Break, by The Rinehart Children

We woke up at 5a.m. Saturday morning for our flight to Ft. Myers, Florida. We were so excited to visit our grandparents in their new Over 55 Active Lifestyle Community. My uncle accidentally called it a Retirement Community when he visited them last month and we haven't heard from him since.

Anyhow, we had no idea our mother could be vertical that early let alone complete a coherent sentence.

You should have seen the look on her face when we knocked on her bathroom door and told her the dog ran away. It was pitch-black outside and we had precisely 9.2 minutes before we had to leave for the airport. Dark circles and deep lines surrounded her eyes and her lips started to twitch. Oh wait, she always looks like that before make-up and coffee.

Mom told us to brush our backpacks and load our teeth in the van while she poured way too much soap in the dishwasher. Then she scrawled big desperate notes for the dog sitter while muttering something about stupid hounds, ingrates and sedatives.

En route to the airport we scanned the dark shoulders of I-85 in the outside chance Hank secretly booked a seat on our flight to surprise us. After we got through security, dad handed mom a twenty and said, "Don't skimp." Mom emerged from Starbucks with a bit more color in her face.

We got to the gate and saw tons of teenagers. We're not sure what Kumbaya is, but mom and dad swore we were living it when the teenagers started playing their guitars and singing. Mom used dad's phone to call our dog sitter. Just as mom said, "I'm sorry I woke you Gary," her cell phone rang. (That's the number on Hank's tag.) She handed dad his phone, answered hers and looked relieved. For about two seconds.

Groveling on very little sleep or coffee, mom told the caller she was in the airport and could they please keep the dog until we could get someone over there. The answer was, "No, my dad hates dogs." Mom started crying and handed her phone to dad.

So there's dad with two phones, trying to write down an address on the A Section of the Independent Tribune while a lady at the next gate stared at mom and Kumbaya continued playing in the background.

Dad, being dad, got it all worked out. Gary, being a saint, went to get Hank (not a saint). Mom drank her coffee, blew her nose and muttered about beagle farms, thick chains and sedatives.

We got excited about the trip again when it was our turn to board the plane. Then mom's ticket wouldn't scan. She was pulled aside for another security check. She started crying again. We pleaded with the gate agent, "Do we have time to run back to Starbucks?"

The New Year

New Year's resolutions. Who invented those nasty things anyhow? And does anyone really take them seriously any time of the year beyond, oh, January 27th?

Back in the dark ages when I was an aerobics instructor (scary, I know) I didn't need a calendar or a cheap champagne headache to know it was the beginning of January. Every single gym member and their conscience showed up for class. Easter and Christmas church services were the only two other times a year when I'd see that many good intentions and sweat in one room.

If you were a faithful attendee, you griped about having to get there early to claim your mat, weights and spot in class. You griped about the Twice-A-Yearers clogging up the parking lot and messing up the routine. They were easy to peg too – not quite knowing when to sit, stand or shut up.

And just like Easter and Christmas, there were all the new outfits. Leotards and bike shorts with elastic that still snapped back. T-shirts without blood and sweat stains on them. Athletic shoes that still had tread on the bottom. Clean white matched socks. Water bottles that had the original spring water in them, not a refill from the tap. Bottle labels weren't bleached or worn off from the dishwasher either.

Like the pews in church come February, the rows of exercise mats would thin and the fights over the 3-pound dumbbells ceased. Pretty soon the year's new faithful had their favorite spots in the room, knew all the steps and had the words to the songs memorized. All was peaceful until the onslaught of bathing suit weather.

I've long since given up any type of resolution that has to do with exercise. I think I lost my interest in the whole scene when I stopped getting paid to jump around and make people sweat. Though ask some of the Bus Stop Mommies and they'll say, "You haven't seen her up at the corner in the mornings!"

Besides, it's so confusing to know who to believe and what new plan to follow for diet, nutrition and exercise. For the past week I've saved newspaper and magazine clippings that mentioned anything about such topics. They're everywhere.

On a coupon page for Slim-Fast: "Resolution Solution. Save $5 now!" How about if you just give me five bucks and let me eat real food?

On another coupon page: "Take the Special K2-Week Challenge! It Works! 2 Bowls a Day. 2 Weeks. Lose up to 6 lbs." Yum.

The cover of Reader's Digest: "Diet Breakthrough. Lose Weight Your Way. Don't Count Calories. Eat the Foods You Like. Feel Better All Over."

That was my favorite until I read the next cover story, "PLUS Make Cash Doing What You Love."

This is going to be a great year.

Transportation and Travel

Thanksgiving Road Trip 2002

Trash bags? Check. Toiletry bags? Check. Food bags? Check. Barf bags? Check. And if I actually need one I'll kill myself. Thankfully motion sickness is one trait with which my children were not blessed. Packing the minivan for a trip Ohio is taxing enough without having to worry about who gets 'shotgun' during the most mountainous section of the journey. So why the barf bag? Past experience my dear, past experience.

"I'm never eating at Wendy's again! I barfed last time we ate there." The kid was eight years old at the time, yet we still have to hear this story every trip we take. "That's because you ate an entire tin of popcorn before we ever got to Wendy's, you freak.!" That kid was five and has the memory of a steel trap...at least when it benefits her. I miss the days when Santa Claus was coming to town and my kids behaved accordingly.

(Editor's note: if anyone was going to give my kids one of those huge tins containing three different flavors of popcorn...please don't.)

I'm starting to doubt the brilliance of planning this trip to Ohio for the Thanksgiving holidays. Anytime my kids have more than a day off from school, I get restless. I also forget that my husband's work schedule doesn't coincide with the school bus schedule. (Life can be so cruel.) So here we are planning on having the van packed and ready to roll as soon as Scott gets home Tuesday evening. That will get us to my brother's back door at the sensible hour of say...oh...2 a.m.

It seemed like a good idea four weeks ago. When it wasn't snowing and sleeting in Columbus, the kids didn't have three projects and a Tuesday morning orthodontist appointment on the calendar and I hadn't agreed to spend half the day at school carving Ivory soap and gluing pilgrim puppets with an unpacked minivan out in the parking lot.

Speaking of packing the van...let me get back to my list. Windshield deicer spray and scraper? Check. Extra blankets, parkas, gloves, hats, flashlights, bunjee cords, cat litter, flares, batteries and magnetic board games? Check. Oh dear, where is Martha and her checklist for every well-prepared trunk when I need her? TV/VCR with cigar lighter plug? Broken. That's it. Trip cancelled. No wait, call and beg to borrow the neighbor's. They're staying in town.

Igloo cooler, greenbeans, Durkee Onions, mushroom soup, wine and nuts?

Check. At this juncture it pains me to admit that I have (again) become my mother…or is it my grandmother? And if they're from different sides of the family, does it count? Anyhow, this time the warning sign is traveling across three states for a holiday dinner and bringing my own ingredients. For my grandmother, I understood it. She made homemade ravioli, Italian sausage, red sauce and sour cream cookies. It wasn't a family holiday without her food no matter where we ate.

My mother, notorious for buying way too much food even after all four kids moved out, has to bring food with her or 'it would go bad'. Plus, she has a surplus of Gift Food—food you never make, eat or realize it exists unless it's a holiday. Sugar-coated pecans, cookies with pecans stuck in the middle of them, pecan peanut brittle and pecan pate. Please don't tell her I still have frosted pecans in my freezer from last year. I must remember to get them out and take them to my sister-in-law.

This would be the sister-in-law who e-mailed me, "Don't bring the green bean casserole ingredients with you. We'll go shopping when you get here." I wrote back and assured her there is not now, nor will there ever be, enough Prozac produced on the Western Hemisphere to make me go Krogering on the Wednesday before Thanksgiving.

Ibuprofen, Alka Seltzer, Tums? Check.

In-Flight Meals

Have you noticed the big brouhaha among the airlines lately? I'm not talking about bomb threats, bankruptcy, luggage searches, or soaring gas prices. This is something much more important.

Food.

That's right. The hot story burning news wires concerns major airlines and in-flight food. Who knew that eliminating six peanuts and eight ounces of bad coffee could save a worldwide conglomerate from financial ruin?

A recent television news exposé portrayed corporate executives and frequent fliers alike flailing about in ash and sackcloth over culinary cutbacks. A prominent airline CEO reported to authorities that he walked into the executive loo to find, "It's the pretzels or you. We can't afford both" scrawled on the stall.

One scene showed an airline employee attempting to calm a first class passenger who just learned he'd be served a cold salad instead of the expected hot lunch. "Whataya mean no hot meal? Are you crazy? First you stopped giving out playing cards. Then it was the pin on wings. But the day you stopped serving plastic cocktail swords – well, I didn't think you could stoop any lower!"

According to one newspaper article, major airlines and their cocktail onion spearing customers are indeed faced with desperate times. "With the industry in its worst-ever tailspin, airlines appear willing to try almost anything to help the bottom line…" That's right, major airlines might start dropping and/or charging for our snacks and meals.

Thinking of flying from Charlotte to Phoenix? If memory serves me, it's about four hours nonstop. Chances are during that length of time you'll get hungry. Or at least eat anything they put in front of you simply to pass the time.

Let's say you're on that Charlotte-Phoenix flight with an airline that now charges for meals. A hot lunch will cost you ten bucks. Before you throw your Kaiser roll at the flight attendant in protest, bear in mind this ten-dollar meal is served on china and includes dessert. The big question remains, do you get a knife to cut the chicken Kiev or must you get by with the fingernail clippers you sneaked on board disguised as bra under-wire. And if someone doesn't wear a bra, where do they hide their fingernail clippers?

On the same route, a cold breakfast of cereal and fruit will cost you eight dollars. No word if coffee is included, how bad it tastes, or if it also comes in a china cup. Regardless, my guess is that stir sticks will run you a quarter and unless you take it black, bring another buck or two for the cream and sugar.

Frankly, all this fuss from travelers over in-flight food mystifies me. For a few extra minutes and the same amount of money, I'd rather have a Cinnamon and Starbucks Extra Tall from the terminal shops. (All the napkins, stir sticks, cream and sugar you can schlep on board included).

Besides, have you ever been seated next to someone during an in-flight meal and heard them exclaim, "This is the best pressed ham and processed cheese I've ever tasted in my entire life! You gonna finish that?"

Trip Preparation: Husband vs. Wife

Please don't hate me. I'm going away with my husband. Alone. No children. To a warm sunny climate. To a warm sunny climate where the hotel is paid for by the company for whom my husband will be working all day, leaving me with nothing better to do than lounge by the pool for three days straight.

I'm not excited. That won't happen until I'm actually parked on said pool chair, but by then I'll be too exhausted from preparing for this trip that I won't remember what it was I was supposed to be excited about.

For four weeks prior to this trip I will do the following:

Bribe, beg or call in the mother of all favors to arrange childcare for my kids; make lists; try on every bathing suit and piece of clothing from last summer; start drastic diet; contemplate tanning booth; grocery shop, make and freeze lasagnas for families taking care of my kids plus one for church supper scheduled for two days before departure...

Change dental appointments made six months prior that fall on the Tuesday I'm gone; arrange dog care; try swim suit again; vow to walk more; make another list; make manicure appointment; get permission from Vice Principal for son to take different bus home; arrange rides for kids to extracurricular activities; pay for next week's lessons in advance; pay all bills due while gone; get stressed; eat entire box of Thin Mints; toss vacation bikini onto closet shelf and get out fat suit...

Write and deliver notes to bus drivers, teachers, coaches saying it's okay for sitters to pick up my kids; sort, wash, dry, fold laundry for every family member; put clothes away or into pre-packing inventory piles; shop for extra socks and underwear; retrieve luggage from attic; print and copy trip itineraries for sitters and parents; get stressed, bite nails; cancel manicure appointment...

Purchase travel size toiletries; take dog to vet; write and attach insurance cards to permission forms for sitters to obtain medical care; pick up prescription refills, dry cleaning and cash; attend meeting at one school, work book fair at other; wake in the middle of the night panicked I forgot something; pack kids', husband's and my suitcases; alert neighbors of our absence; arrange for pick up of mail, paper and recycling bin; wash dog's blanket and kid's P.E. uniforms; realize I have nothing to wear; panic; call girlfriend for advice; then stay up until 2 a.m. repacking my bag.

On departure day, after a fitful night's sleep, I'll double-check flight times, put gas in car, adjust thermostat and curtains, scrub toilets, empty trash cans, run dishwasher, load minivan, deliver instructions to dog sitter and kids to respective homes. Put makeup on in car on way to airport.

On departure day, my husband will transfer his sunglasses and briefcase from his car to the pre-packed minivan and drive us to the airport. He'll affectionately slap me on the thigh and cajole, "Come on Honey! Act excited!"

Minivan Mom

Would someone please tell me why I bothered to wash and vacuum the minivan before we went away this weekend? To the mountains, no less! We came home with enough rock samples to make my flowerbeds. With the rocks came rock dust, rock dirt and rock chips. Leaves, sticks, ferns, bugs and muddy shoes? Yup, got those too.

The dog had to be transported to the kennel and back, but I figured I could isolate him to one easy-to-wipe spot. The passenger seat. Outside of the drool and shedding, he's actually a pretty good driving companion. No whining, fighting, sneezing on the back of my head, yelling, 'He touched me!', picking his nose and flinging the contents across the van, kicking the back of my seat, telling me which radio station to turn on or 'Turn it up!'. OK, so there's the small issue of wet nose marks on the window but it's no different from little sticky handprints.

It took me a while to get over my messy van phobia. It took even longer for my ego to get over driving a minivan to begin with – clean or dirty.

I grew up on the flip-up cargo area seat of our wood paneled Ford LTD. My two older brothers got the back seat and my other brother and I got the way back. No seat belts, no rear air vents and all the carbon monoxide we could breathe in through the open rear window.

When I got married and started a family, I swore I'd never ever drive a station wagon. We brought our second child home from the hospital in a Ford Taurus wagon. But it had gray leather interior and a tape deck. Fine, I thought. But I'm never ever going to stoop to the level of Gooberdom by driving a minivan.

We took our second child to her first beach vacation in our brand new metallic gold Pontiac Transport Minivan. But it had a remote control power sliding door, built-in cup holders and a tape deck.

I remember the day I came to be at peace as a Minivan Mom. I was cruising up Florida US 1 in my metallic gold Pontiac, feeling like I was on top of the world. (It was more like four feet off the ground in a bucket seat). At a stoplight, I glanced to my left and looked down on a complete vision. A handsome man, about my age, in a fire engine red Mazda Miata, top down and, get this, a rosary hanging on his rearview mirror.

I shifted in my seat and put on my perkiest "Wow, She Looks Great For A Woman Her Age Who Has Given Birth" pose. Then it hit me. I was looking *down* on this guy. From my minivan. I might as well have been driving an 18-wheeler with tobacco juice dribbling down my chin. My life of catching any ego-boosting glance from a passing motorist or construction worker was over. *Face it*, I told myself; *you are now officially a Goober. Make the best of it.*

Last week I parked my red Chevy minivan next to a Volvo sedan in the Middle School parking lot. There was a baby seat in the back and get this, absolutely nothing, I mean nothing else in that car. No toys, dog hair, juice boxes, half eaten suckers or boogers. Not even a lipstick-smeared coffee mug in the front.

I heard someone yell, "Holy Freak Of Nature! Call Children's Services! What kind of weirdo drives a child around in a perfectly clean vehicle?" Wait. It was me. Oh no. Was I not as secure in my minivan life as I thought I was? Was I secretly envious of the Volvo driver with the clean car? I have been drooling lately at the sight of BMW convertibles. (I want metallic ice blue with tan interior.)

Nah. I already have a tan leather interior. Covered in inkblots and sticky mystery goo. Plus broken cup holders, a power sliding door and cassette player.

And priceless dog art on the windows.

This column appeared on www.flighthumor.org and sparked a few spirited responses. Did you know Wilbur was born in Indiana?

The Wright Stuff

I believe in miracles. First, my 13-year-old son acknowledged my presence in front of his peers during a class trip. Second, you have this column. Over three days I logged a thousand miles on my minivan and four hours of uninterrupted sleep at the Bates Motel. I was suffering from severe Starbucks withdrawal and tired-brain-writer's block.

As any Bus Stop Mommy knows, you don't have to chaperone an out-of-town field trip to feel tired and stupid. Childbirth does this for you. The more educated our kids get the harder it is to look good in their eyes. How are we supposed to know there is a new way to carry the one when multiplying double digits? Or that Creed is a rock group and not something we recite at Mass every week?

So when my kids simultaneously studied aviation history, I got excited about dinnertime conversations that wouldn't put me on the same intellectual level as my dog. Schooled in Ohio, I was saturated in aviation history and trained to take great pride in my homeland pioneers: Neil Armstrong, John Glenn and Dayton's native sons, the Wright brothers.

I was taught I lived in the land of the Wrights, but now my kids are being taught they live in the Wright Place. I saw North Carolina's claim manifested first hand on the field trip with a scheduled stop to the Wright Brothers' Memorial. High atop a grassy hill sits a giant cement cone complete with massive ornately carved nickel doors. One kid, who had previously seen Napoleon's tomb, asked if the brothers were buried there.

"No, they're buried in Dayton, Ohio. Where they were raised, designed, built and tested their planes. They merely flew near this spot because the weather conditions were favorable." I made it back to the bus before being trampled by angry native North Carolinians.

Meanwhile, back at the ranch, the dinner debate became lively. Spoons were banged, voices raised and much to the dog's delight, food started to fly. I understand this is similar to the behavior in both Ohio and North Carolina's legislative lunchrooms when the same debate raged. Minus the dog, so I guess they had to clean up after themselves.

Both states claim ownership to the origin of flight so strongly that they produced license plates to prove it. Ohio's plates read, 'Birthplace of Aviation' while North Carolina's say, 'First In Flight'. Both Dayton and The Outerbanks have Centennial of Flight celebrations planned for Summer, 2003.

What's a mother to do? Prove my children wrong, naturally. Luckily, a colleague came to my rescue with the following: www.flighthumor.org. As a parent, he knew my kids would believe something flashing colorfully on a screen, even if it's exactly what I just told them in spoken English.

So gather your family around; check out the site; view the (G-rated) movie clip and let the dinner table debate begin. Let me know your pick for the Wrightful claimant…and if you need to borrow my dog.

The Personal Family Chauffeur
(And I Don't Mean You or Me)

You've heard other women say it. You've probably said it yourself. "I need more hours in the day. I need some help around here. I need thinner thighs. I need the ability to be in three places at once." What we need, dear friends, is a Personal Family Chauffeur.

As my kids age and become more involved in extracurricular activities, the more I'm tempted to sacrifice the chocolate budget for a Family Chauffeur budget. I know I have it a lot easier than most of you – my kids only participate in two scheduled activities each per week – but even with a light social schedule, I still end up needing to be three places at once.

The two times a year the middle school hosts Parent Nights, they'll inevitably fall on the two Mondays of the month that my son's volunteer civic duties coincide with my daughter's horseback riding which coincides with my husband's biannual board meeting. It's also the Monday the dog will run away, the meat I defrosted for dinner goes bad and I'll have cramps.

The third Saturday night of the month when the youth group meets will be the Saturday my husband is out of town, it sleets in October and my daughter gets the flu.

The second Saturday of the month when my daughter has horse shows will be the Saturday the race is in town, my husband is working, the horse farm hosts their annual picnic and my son has the flu.

"But Karen, my family already has a chauffeur: Me." Yes I know; we're all in the same boat er, minivan er, SUV… but wouldn't it be true luxury to have someone cart your kids around for you? Someone as trustworthy and dependable as Grandma but with sharper vision and faster reflexes.

The Bus Stop Mommies brainstormed and listed luxury services available to housewives these days. Then I posed this question to myself: "Self? If you had the money to put towards one of these services, would you pick any of them over a Personal Family Chauffeur?" Here are my uncensored thoughts, straight from my road wary brain to yours.

Dry Cleaning Home Pick Up and Delivery: Oh good gawd no way. I share enough dirty laundry in this column that I don't need to hang it on my front porch too.

Maid Service: This is a tough one. I'm squinting through unidentifiable smears on this monitor screen and I have a well known phobia towards mopping. It's not that I'd slam the door on one if she (or he!) appeared on my front porch and said, "Hi! I'm highly qualified, honest, hardworking, inexpensive, licensed, bonded and insured. I do windows, scrub the floor behind toilets and bring my own lunch."

I'm just not sure I want a perfect stranger emptying my trashcans. You can learn a lot about someone that way.... Plus, I'd have to clear a path through the kids' rooms and bathrooms before the maid could ever begin the actual cleaning. I think I'd rather scrub my toilets by the light of day and pay the PFC to drive across town to the church gym in the pouring rain at 10 p.m. Saturday to pick up a van load of sweaty teenage boys.

Window Washer: They're supposed to be washed? On both sides? Whose sick idea was that?

Lawn Service: There is no way my husband would let me pay someone else to mow our lawn. If we farmed out this chore, my teenage son's entire reason for existence would be gone. When my son was born, my brother gave him a set of miniature golf clubs. My husband gave him a toy lawn mower.

I honestly don't mind my part in the yard care either. Edging the driveway gives me instant satisfaction and the results last longer than a good eyebrow waxing. I simultaneously get my exercise and a tan.

Digging in the dirt, pulling weeds and pruning trees is cheap therapy. Frankly, pulling the ripcord on those gas-powered tools is just plain fun; not to mention the only time I have the power to frighten my dog into obedience.

Interior Designer/Home Decorating: What? And miss an opportunity to go shopping? Think not.

Grocery Delivery: What? And miss the free food samples at BJ's? Think not.

Car Wash: Again, this is why I have children. Heck, even the neighbor kid came over the other day and asked if he could help wash the van. "I love to do this!" he exclaimed while my own son, his friend, was hiding indoors. "Uh, OK. Knock yourself out. But I get to vacuum. You're crazy if you think I'm going to give up finder's keepers on all the loose change in the seats."

Dog Grooming: Our dog's grooming consists of bathing and nail clipping. Again: children. The exception to this was when Hank was a puppy. Anyone who attempted nail clipping without the benefit of anesthesia or at least three linebackers holding him down, came out looking like raw hamburger on a butcher's bad day.

Personal Chef: OK this one's the most tempting so far. Waking up on Monday morning knowing the freezer was full of ready-to-bake meals gives me goose bumps. But knowing me I'd forget to defrost them in time, so why bother.

I wonder if that limo guy in town would cut us moms a deal....

My Glamorous Life

My neighbors called me Cindy for weeks after this ran.

Domestic Cinderella Complex

It's widely known we housewives have been setting major fashion trends for centuries—going to the bus stop and school parking lot in our pajamas, elevating yoga attire to debutante status and forcing sweat pants manufacturers to break out beyond basic navy and athletic gray.

As a young housewife and mother, I made a conscious effort to look pulled together when I went out in public. I had a duty-like need to show that moms did not become hapless fashion hags once they started staying home with kids. The sweats came off; the slacks went on. The hair came down; the makeup went on.

14 years later I've loosened up a bit. OK, a lot. To the point that I practically embarrass myself, let alone my family, with the way I look. I met a mom in the produce section at Wal-Mart the other day and I swear the only reason she recognized me was that I'd just come from getting my haircut. Had it been the day before, the whole un-blow-dried mess would have been tucked under my Marines.com hat and I'd have been dressed and ready for yard work.

I've come home from running errands, passed myself in the mirror and thought, "Oh my gawd, I just went out in public looking like THAT? What's happened to me?"

I'll tell you what's happened. Life. Kids. Kids and life getting busier than ever. Kids and life making me older and wiser, which makes my ego a little less fragile. This being the same ego that never would have allowed a younger me to go through a pharmacy drive through at night in a foreign city without a full face of make up.

About 364 days of the year I'm perfectly content to exist in blue jeans and clogs. It doesn't bother me that the fanciest fabric in my wardrobe is a 5 percent Lycra / 95 percent cotton blend. And I truly don't mind that I wear more dog hair than mohair.

So why did I get so upset when my husband told me he's going to another black tie business affair next month? In New York City. At the Waldorf Astoria.

Is it because I'll be home with the kids studying for end of semester exams, watching primetime reruns and trying to keep the dog from eating all the lower Christmas tree ornaments? I think it boils down to the Domestic Cinderella Complex.

Once. Just once I want to put on something that requires dry cleaning. And Specialty Dry-Cleaning at that. I want a bigger reason than a parent-teacher conference to put on make-up. (Then it's mostly concealer to hide the dark circles I got from staying up all night with worry.)

I want a better reason than smiling at the dog to bleach my teeth. Remember the marching in the rain scene from Private Benjamin? "I want to go out to lunch. I want to wear sandals. I want to be normal again." I'm with you there, Goldie.

I want an excuse to get all prettied up again. I want an excuse to complain about shoes hurting my feet, the 12 shades of nude hose and how no amount of control top is really ever enough. I want a reason to eat nothing but celery and water for three days in order to fit into a dress.

I want to actually see my husband in his tuxedo and not just drive it back and forth to the cleaners. I want to go to an event and see chandeliers that don't need dusting, pretty things and pretty people and pretty dishes.

For just one evening, I want to carry a purse that isn't big enough to hold soccer cleats, diapers and a six-pack of Slim Fast. I want to sit at dinner where everyone at my table uses utensils. For their food.

I need a reason to suck in my stomach other than the family Christmas picture and meeting the old girlfriend. I want to have the door of a taxi held open; so for a brief moment in time I'm Audrey Hepburn and not June Cleaver.

I want the glass slipper, footman and my prince.

For just one night.

My Glamorous Housewife Life

I live the ultimate glamorous life: I am a Housewife. If you are a fellow housewife and your response to me is, "Yeah, right, glamorous my perpetually spreading fanny!" you are 1. Probably reading this in the bathroom 2. Obviously missing the glamour in your own daily routine and 3. In need of my warped insight so you too can feel worthy to be on the cover of a magazine other than Ranger Rick.

Why, just this morning I was simultaneously being caressed by pulsating jets of therapeutic aquasubstantialoxide, perfecting an advanced Yoga maneuver and receiving a spa pedicure.

OK, I was bent over in the shower picking the faded red nail polish off my toes. But hey, let's look at the upside, or shall I say *glamorside,* of this scenario:

* At age 37 I'm still able to bend over and reach my toes.
* I own red nail polish and I'm not afraid to use it.
* The hot water and yoga-ish stretch felt wonderful on my aching lower back.
* I sound trendy, hip and modern because now I can honestly say, "I do yoga."
* The dog, for once, did not stick his tongue under the shower doors for a drink.
* I was alone in my own home, able to take a twenty-minute shower without anyone barging in screaming, "Maaawm, he looked at me!"

How much more glamour can a girl want? Well, a spa vacation in Tucson would be nice thank you very much. But then my practical side thinks of all the paint, draperies and baby sitters I could buy with that $2000. (Not to mention the fact that we don't have a spare $2000.) Instead of Tucson, I'll relish every moment of an occasional massage here in town. My husband has come to realize that $50 is a small investment towards warding off my stress induced tantrums. He hasn't squawked about my annual pre-sandal season pedicure either. Of course he doesn't know about it yet.

The point is, if this Plain Jane can occasionally don her Glamour Woman cape, you too can find the glamour and beautiful perks of the housewife life. You've probably already enjoyed such moments without realizing it. I recently had one of those completely euphoric moments of total freedom and bliss that only housewife life can provide.

The smells of spring filled my back yard. I was wearing my favorite faded, blue jeans, my sexy Italian shoes and a new shirt. The sun warmed my blemish-free face and the breeze blew through my shiny hair. Translated: I was picking up dog poop and flinging it into the woods behind my house; those are the only jeans that fit me; the shirt was a Salvation Army find. My skin is only clear after six months of nasal drying, lip cracking prescriptions and I used the shampoo from the horse farm.

"Um, Karen, where is the glamour in all this?" I'll tell you—the handle on the shovel was so long I didn't have to smell the poop. Time was totally mine. The kids were in school; I had nowhere to go; no one to whom I had to answer; no errands to run and no dinner to plan, thanks to the motherload of leftovers in the fridge. I could talk to myself and no one talked back. No repeating, correcting, or justifying. Now that is luxury and luxury is glamour and I'm going to stop now while no one is currently spitting up on me and I still believe all this.

One woman wrote and said she'd been using the Pine-Sol trick for over a decade.

What Did You Do Today?

Years ago, back before I had a dishwasher and second child, I read an article in one of those women's magazines about cheating on housework. It went something along the lines of: "How to make your husband think you've been cleaning and working hard all day when you really haven't."

One lady's tip was to pour Pine Sol down the kitchen drain before her husband got home from work. She swore it made the house smell like she'd been cleaning all day long. I remember thinking, *Well, that's stupid! Wouldn't her husband be able to look around and see that the house wasn't really clean? And why would she need to fake it anyhow? Wasn't staying home with the children work enough without justifying how her time was spent?*

Boy was I naïve back then. Let me tell you, I have come to love Pine Sol and its scent is often wafting through our home when my husband arrives from work. It's particularly handy now that both our kids are school aged and come supper time, when I'm struggling to figure out what supper will actually be, my husband walks in and asks, "So, what did you do today?" This is only second in annoying to him asking, before my second cup of coffee, "So, what are you doing today?"

In a panic I search my cloudy brain for a list that sounds productive, certain not to use the words Bon Bons, Soap Opera or Nap. Some days, no matter how productive I've been, I can't think of a thing to say when he asks. The things I do are often indescribable when I open my mouth to speak.

Take yesterday for example. I grabbed the dishrag to wipe up a glob of melted three-day-old mint chocolate chip ice cream off the kitchen floor. Would you believe those chocolate chips were as solid and minty as ever? Before I stood up again, I had scrubbed the entire kitchen floor on my hands and knees with the wimpy little dishrag. The two-inch gap between the refrigerator and the cabinet never looked so good.

Now my knees hurt. Thinking I had some Ben Gay in my bathroom, I headed in that direction. I never made it. I spotted "I hate my brother!"

written in the dust on the bookcases in the foyer and started dusting them with the bottom half of my "I Love My Children" T-shirt.

I picked up the picture of my brother and remembered that I still had scrapbook pages to compile for his birthday. Ten minutes later I located the scrapbook materials in the back corner of my closet, underneath the sandals I got on sale two summers ago and forgot I owned.

That reminded me, where was the shirt I bought last week? I started digging through the hanging items and realized I never wore half the stuff anymore. The urge to purge struck and when it strikes, you just have to go with it. The next two hours were spent trying on clothes I forgot I owned since they were on the bottom of my 8-foot tall To Be Mended/Altered pile. I divided items into bags labeled, Give Away, Take To Consignment, Give Back To Original Owner and What Is This And Please Tell Me I Didn't Actually Pay Money For It.

I hauled the bags out to the van and glanced at my herb garden. When was the last time I fertilized it? As I was mixing the blue stuff, the bus arrived and my children announced they needed poster boards and a working volcano by morning. We sped off to K-Mart for the project supplies. I picked up two gallons of Pine Sol.

One Easy To Please Woman Or Just Plain Boring

My son popped his head in the door, "Mom, can we play with the stuff in this box?"

"Sure. Go away."

"Even this black stuff and the bubble wrap?"

"Yes. Now fly, be free."

Soon the melodious sounds of popping bubble wrap filled the air. My neighbors working out in their yard dove for cover while the folks behind us called and asked what I fed the kids for dinner last night.

I'm sitting here listening to my kids play out in the garage. Our back door is not as soundproof as I thought it'd be which can be a good thing or a bad thing. Bad, because I can hear everything they're doing as I try to concentrate on getting this column written. Good, because I can hear everything they're doing since they're my children.

I wonder if the fascination with bubble wrap is a genetic condition. When my three brothers and I were little, we would fight to the point of bloodshed over who got to pop the bubble wrap that occasionally arrived in the mail. Just this past weekend I watched my brother open presents on his 40th birthday. As he reached his hand into one bag, his face lit up with joy and he exclaimed, "WOOO HOOO! BUBBLE WRAP!" I don't remember the actual gift.

My parents raised us to be rather low maintenance, easy to please children and my husband, I know, is grateful. I mean, it just doesn't take much to get me excited or make me happy.

For some women I know, happiness means a new diamond bracelet, a cruise to the islands or a husband home from work carrying a dozen roses. Not that I would turn these down, but for me, just my husband making it home each day is enough. Well, coming home before 7 p.m. is good. And quizzing the kids for tomorrow's tests…then cleaning up the kitchen after dinner and ironing his own shirts… no it doesn't take much to please me.

Why, just look at all the exciting things that float my boat on this sea called domesticity.

* Opening the dryer in dreaded anticipation of endless folding and finding it empty
* Transferring clothes from the washer into the dryer before they mildew

* Opening the dishwasher and finding it empty
* Enough creamer left in the carton for my Monday morning coffee
* Hearing these words while pushing a full cart of groceries, realizing I have precisely 13 minutes to get home before the bus arrives, "I can take you on lane 4 with no waiting."
* Matching a load of socks without one leftover
* Kids who tie their own shoes
* Finding something right where I left it
* Getting through a week without a child telling me they're out of clean underwear
* Getting through a week without a child telling me at 10 p.m. they need poster board to complete a project due tomorrow
* Discovering my back door was magnetic
* Discovering my refrigerator is white now that my back door is covered with artwork, etc.
* Underwear that doesn't ride up
* Getting the dog outside during the gagging stage, prior to the barfing stage
* Craving something sweet and finding the candy bar I hid behind the Brussels sprouts
* A friend for my child
* A box (not bottle) of Mr. Bubble that is mine, all mine
* Locating a pen without dumping the contents of my purse
* Getting email that doesn't start out, "FWD. FWD. FWD. FWD. FWD. FWD."
* Come spring realizing I didn't plant my tulip bulbs upside down again

So there you have it – one easy to please (or incredibly boring) woman. My husband will agree with me…right honey? Honey? Sweetie? Hello?

The Meeting

"So how will I know it's you?" he wrote. "Will you be wearing a hat? Cowboy boots?" I sat there staring at the e-mail, typing a reply, then erasing it. Typing another sentence, then erasing it. I had no clue where to begin. I've not needed to describe my physical appearance to a stranger since, oh, the summer after ninth grade, when a well-meaning friend stuck a phone in my hand and said, "Go for it! He's cute and he's the best friend of the brother of my boyfriend's neighbor's friend."

There I was at the age of 37, a happily married woman, mother and downright domestic diva, arranging a meeting (1) With a man I'd never met. (2) At a bar (3) Three states away. And yes, my husband knew all about it, as did this guy's wife.

Okay, okay, I was arranging a professional meeting with another newspaper columnist. Who lives in my hometown near Columbus, Ohio. Plus he knows my brother and coached my niece in soccer. My sister-in-law knows his wife. It was as safe and professional a meeting as there could be. Except for the trick of recognizing each other.

I had a vague idea of what he looked like from an outdated, grainy, black and white newspaper photo. He'd never seen my outdated grainy, black and white newspaper photo, hence, the laughable job of trying to describe myself. I settled for, "I'm a shorter, more feminine version of my brother Jimmy and after checking the weather reports, will be wearing a gray wool coat and black bucket hat. Count on highly stylish yet totally impractical boots."

Now with such a stellar, graphic description like that, is it any wonder we sat at the same restaurant for an hour and a half and never found each other?

I'm happy to say we eventually got together a few days later. Beforehand, I studied his color photo on a website and phoned him at work to tell me the exact chair in which he'd be sitting and what he was wearing. "First chair at the top of the steps and a navy blazer under my trench coat." Great. Now I was walking blindly into a bar three states away looking for a married man in a trench coat.

I walked into the restaurant and saw a semi-familiar looking guy on the first chair at the top of the stairs. Check. I spied a trench coat over the back of his chair. Check. Navy blazer? Check. After shaking hands and profusely re-apologizing to each other for the previous mix up, he said, "I swear there are at least six people here that I want to introduce you to, to prove you're real." Seems my colleague got some strange looks and comments the other night. I passed on the offer.

It turned out to be time well spent, sharing ideas on columns, books and most effective methods for not embarrassing our children in public. The most important conclusion to come out of this whole fiasco is this: Our spouses will never have to worry about either one of us running away with anyone we meet online.

We'd never find each other.

Domestic Bliss

My Other Home: The Laundry Room

"Do you ever stop?" asked my dad, with a hint of *I could find a better way to do it better* in his voice. "No Dad, I don't. This is the first place I shuffle to when I wake up in the morning and the last thing I see before I go to bed at night."

I wish I could tell you we were standing in front of a plate full of powder sugar sprinkled brownies, my children's sleeping faces or even something as noble as a crucifix in my private home chapel, but no. It was an endless stack of dirty clothes in the laundry room.

Every Bus Stop Mommy knows that a day without laundry is the day your son needs clean gym clothes, your husband runs out of boxers and your daughter's life will be ruined if she can't wear her favorite khaki shorts and blue t-shirt.

I'm one of those women that has to do at least one load of laundry every day or I get overwhelmed with the accumulation. Some women save it all for one marathon day. This would not only make me insane but also force me to go out and buy 82 more pairs of socks and underwear for every member of my household.

In my old house, the one car garage became my laundry room. Though it shared its austere title with those of Workshop, Storage Shed, Bike Depot, and Roach Motel, I didn't mind. What used to be the indoor laundry space became a large closet for me, me, me. I'd have done laundry in a barrel in the back yard in exchange for that closet.

As far as laundry rooms go, the garage version was rather deluxe. I had a utility sink; whose presence I mourn to this day, floor space for laundry baskets, counter space for folding, swanky fluorescent light fixtures and ample hanging space on the old metal garage door.

With carpet on the floor, I could haul all the dirties out to the garage and sort them into piles. I'd entertain myself by awarding points for 'closest to the heap' and 'dead on' shots. Wait. Maybe I shouldn't admit that.

The garage space was also handy for enacting the lifesaving Toss It, Slam It and Worry About It Later trick. (Think: The in-laws are at the door and you're holding the remnants of potty training accidents and under-the-bed discoveries.)

My current laundry room, and I use that term loosely, is a sliver smaller than a Volkswagen Bug. No hanging space, no folding space, nada. It has a window so small I don't bother to lock it. No burglar could fit through it unless he brought his toddler as an accomplice. You know those spiffy plastic drawer units designed to fit in between the washer and dryer? No room for that either.

This 'room', for lack of a better word, sits right off the back entry into my kitchen. If you come over, expect to step over and through piles of dirty clothes, as the kitchen floor is my new sorting kingdom. As inconvenient as it seems, it scores high on the list of How To Look Like You've Been Working Hard All Day Even Though It Never Shows strategies.

My friend Amy has the Taj Mahal of laundry rooms. First, it's upstairs, so she doesn't have to haul dirties all over the house. Second, the whole room is the size of my first house. Not only does she have counter space for folding clothes and making coffee, she has room underneath for a mini fridge, icemaker, trash compactor, wine cooler and snack storage. On the opposite wall, she has more hanging space than the neighborhood dry cleaners.

If she weren't my friend, I'd hate her. Maybe she'll let me bring my laundry over to her house for a small fee…like a can of spray starch and a '98 Chardonnay.

The New Iron

The kids are home on a snow day. The 4th one this winter has landed on a Friday before a Monday holiday. The fourth snow day has created a four-day weekend and I have four extra kids in my house.

There's only one thing outside of the stomach flu that could fit the mood I'm in. Ironing. I got out the board, spray starch, water bottle and iron. Then I brewed a pot of strong coffee, gathered a stack of DVD's and the portable phone. Now I'm sitting here working on this column with the ironing set up just inside my peripheral vision.

Have I told you how much I hate to iron? Which is really inconvenient since everything my husband wears to work requires ironing. Fortunately, Scott is quite skilled with an iron and can press his entire wardrobe during the first quarter of Monday night football. I'd be ironing the same load straight through till baseball season.

So if he's so good at it, why am I torturing myself, right? It's my Domestic Guilt Syndrome. He's at work all day in order to put food on the table and keep water running out of the tap so I can make meals and fill this iron. I, on the other hand, have the luxury of time during the day to do fun, carefree stuff like shopping for and preparing the food and cleaning said tap. And to iron.

Yes, I know there are several qualified dry cleaners that would love to do the work for me; but basically, we're cheap. Add that to the Domestic Guilt and here I sit on a beautiful sunny snow-glistening day next to a basket of crumpled Wrinkle Free Dockers.

The only thing making today's endeavor a little more exciting is my new iron. It was a birthday gift from my mom and dad. Here's the sad part: I was so excited when I opened it, you'd have thought they gave me a BMW. Although like a BMW, it's made and designed in Germany with lots of shiny chrome, plus buttons labeled with symbols instead of words.

Desperate to stall longer, I read the instruction book. You've got to love an iron that requires tap water only and insists you never use the self-cleaning feature more than once a month. This iron was born to live with my ironing board and me.

The oversized, extra wide board was made in Italy and features a fold down sleeve arm and shelf 'for folded clothing'. I use it for my TV controller and snacks. After I suffer the anguish of ironing a pair of pants two times taller than me, I don't fold them. Those puppies go straight on a hanger and in the closet for safekeeping.

I suppose if I really let my imagination go wild, I could convince myself of the romance in all this European engineered equipment and make the whole task much more pleasant.

Yeah, right.

Spring Cleaning

Dear Karen,
I'm so happy that spring is in the air—I'm even looking forward to
spring-cleaning! At Home Made Simple this month, we're enjoying the
burst of energy and inspiration—and we hope you are, too.
Best Wishes, Julie B.

And so begins another highly personal, newsy e-mail from my overflow-ing inbox. It was in there with similarly personal notes from Orbitz Travel Advisor, U.S. Airways, Population Research Institute, Proctor and Gamble, my insurance company and Dudu Bensen, the Personal Assistant to the Late Congo President, Lurent Kabila, who "is writing to me because of the need for a trusted and honest person, with whom he can entrust the sum of US$62,800,000."

But back to my close friend Julie B. Last month she gave me tips on cleaning out my refrigerator. I stopped reading when she wrote, "First, un-plug the unit and remove every single item from inside the refrigerator and freezer. You will need to find a place to keep everything cold for a few hours." I got so overwhelmed from just thinking about it, that I sent the letter to my Deal With It When I'm A Bit More Stable file.

The refrigerator can wait. Not too many people actually see the inside of it anyhow. I knew there was a good reason not to replace that burned out bulb. Now the common areas of my house are another story. I can't say I'm currently experiencing Julie B's burst of energy and inspiration… It's what I like to call, Motivation By Desperation.

Yesterday I started to open the family room blinds and noticed someone wrote in the dirt, "Set VCR for 9-11p.m. on Wednesday to record the season finale of 'Help I'm A Celebrity Get Me Out of Here!'" No, I did not mean to say dust. I meant dirt. And debris. And splatters of unidentifiable goo. What are those kids doing in this room? And why did the dog hide behind the couch when I reached for the blind?

I made the mistake of grabbing the damp dishrag. My dirt became mud. This blind cleaning thing would not be a one step process. First I had to vacuum the initial layer of dirt. This revealed the finer layer of dirt plus caked-on goo. Next came the bucket of hot sudsy water, 42 rags, the stepladder and a box of Band-Aids. (If you have to ask what the Band-Aids are for, you've never before, God bless you, had to clean a horizontal blind.)

After creating a nice bucket full of muddy water that even our grass-eating-toilet-water-drinking dog wouldn't touch, it was time for the Goo Gone. You know, that citrus smelling stuff that no mother should be without. Translated: it works on removing crayons and gum from your carpet, walls and in-laws' car interior.

An hour later I had two shiny, citrus smelling window blinds. Only twelve more to go! I plopped down on the couch to take a little breather and contemplate changing out of my pajamas before continuing. I leaned my head back, raised my arms up, stretched…and saw the ceiling fans.

Curse Julie B.

Home Made *Simple,* my dustbunnies.

Everything I Know About My Son
I Learned From Emptying His Pockets

I'm writing today's column with the melodic rhythm of the washer, the hypnotic hum of the dryer and mellow scent of chlorine bleach in the air...ah, another day of laundering bliss. I could have sworn the hampers were empty just yesterday, yet here I am sorting out the kids' lights and darks, mildly dirties and don't even bothers.

My son is currently taking the seventh grade class, Life Skills (formally known as Home Economics). I needed to give proof that he completed an assignment, so I wrote this letter:

Dear Mrs. Kelemecz:
This is to inform you that this weekend Morgan Rinehart completed his laundry homework assignment. I supervised him as he gathered the dirty laundry, sorted by fabric weight and color, loaded the washer, made all those exciting decisions like water temperature and wash time, etc. etc...transferred clothes into the dryer, folded and put them away in the proper places. Please be assured that he did the work himself as I was too busy singing praises for you and your Life Skills class.
Thank you, Karen Rinehart.

Shortly thereafter, I attended orientation for the new middle school, where I had the pleasure of meeting the famed Mrs. Kelemecz. I had a strong urge to drop to my knees and kiss her feet, but with the room crowded, I opted to grovel upright. Besides the fact that she's teaching my son to sew, cook, eat nutritiously and launder his own clothes, she's incredibly kind and likes my boy. To me, she ranks right up there with my daughter's bus driver and St. Whirlpool herself.

Perhaps you're wondering why I'm still slaving over my son's laundry now that he knows how to do it himself. Pure and simple it's to maintain what fleeting control I have over my son's life. The boy will be off to college (please God) in five years and I'll no longer have a say in what he wears, the condition of the sheets on his bed or if his underwear is suitable for a car wreck. Besides, being busy with his laundry is another excuse to delay ironing my husband's shirts.

Once viewed as a tedious time consuming chore, I now rather enjoy, even look forward to, emptying his pockets. As a matter of fact, I hope he never empties them again until he's 29 and some sweet girl is doing his laundry for him…at the rectory.

Fast approaching the official start of his teenage years, my son has started acting appropriately—mumbling short grunts when I ask about his day. Emptying my son's pockets is the only way I know what's happening in his life.

If I didn't check the wadded up papers and debris in his pockets, I wouldn't know what he scored on last week's math quiz, what candy he ate, about the skit in social studies class, how many pieces of plastic and springs make up the inside of a ballpoint pen or how short a pencil can be sharpened and still look and function like a pencil. Then there are the archeological finds – knick-knacks and trash get left on school and bus floors just waiting for geologists or my son to collect.

Out of the deep dark depths I've unearthed paper clips, magnets, candle stubs, rubber bands, empty tic-tac containers, pencils, half chewed erasers, spit-wads, hall passes, sticks, rocks, asthma inhalers, the missing calculator, Legos, candy in various stages of consumption, American and foreign currency, staples, bobby pins bent into a new life form and a multitude of unidentifiable untouchables. I should have a hazardous materials clause in my homeowners' policy. On the less dangerous side, I recently pieced together a mangled yet fluffy soft and static free bible verse from his catechism class.

All my digging makes me think: whoever invented cargo pocket pants never did laundry. Have you ever tried to find all 52 pockets on a size 16 pair of kid's pants? How 'bout fitting your hand into the tall narrow pockets designed to hold a pencil or comb but that your child somehow stuffed with something the size of Baltimore?

Please don't ever let me get too close to the non-laundry-doing masochist who added zipper and Velcro to all the cargo pockets. I've fought with jammed and broken pocket zippers before tossing pants into the washer only to burn myself on them fresh out of the dryer. I've picked threads and fuzz out of Velcro patches until my fingers bled. How secure do they think my son's pockets need to be? Are they afraid someone's going to pickpocket him to pawn his pencil stubs?

I suppose the answers to this and many other laundry quandaries will remain a mystery (missing socks to be discussed another day) but this I know for sure: Some weekend, in the not too distant future, my son will come home from college for the weekend, drop garbage bags full of mildewed laundry on my floor, grunt, empty out my refrigerator, then leave to meet his friends.

I'll treasure the time getting to know my son all over again…by emptying his pockets.

The Domino Effect: Cleaning Out The Fridge

I don't know what came over me. It just happened. All I know is one minute I was praying to the light at the rear of the dark tunnel for dinner inspiration and the next minute I was waist deep in seven half-empty mustard jars. I should've never opened that refrigerator door.

When I attempted to move the mayonnaise aside and it stuck to the glass shelf… perhaps that's what made me start cleaning. I pried off the jar, grabbed a rag and attacked the ring of sticky goo. Except the ring became a river and I had to empty half the shelf to get it all. At that point, I figured I might as well remove the shelf and wash it in the sink. It's a lot easier to reach that way, but mainly I feared easing too deep into the fridge lest my kids shove and lock me in until I promised to serve them ice cream for breakfast.

With the shelf removed, all sorts of pretty drips and spatters became visible on the interior walls. I filled the sink with fresh, hot sudsy water and got out the heavy-duty scrubber sponge. What was that stuff and how long was it there? I did some calculating…we were in our old house…it was getting replumbed…the kids were old enough to tell the plumber embarrassing family habits…we still had our old dog because I remember him peeing on the plumber's new truck…Right. We bought this fridge six years ago.

And the remnants of the Energy Efficiency Rating label were still stuck inside. Today was as good as any to clean them off. My heavy-duty scrubber sponge gummed up in one swipe. I got out the 'Goo Gone'. It made the kitchen smell citrus fresh but didn't cut all the way through the adhesive. I shouted out from the cavern, "Hey kids, bring mommy a razor blade, would ya?" I heard them dial the phone. "Dad, remember that time you told us to tell you if mom started playing with sharp objects again?"

Scott made it home in record time but the damage had been done. Each crisper drawer had been removed, scrubbed inside and out and lined with fresh white paper towels. The door shelves had been disassembled, cleaned, dried and replaced. The condiments were arranged by color and bottle size. The leftover Florida grapefruit Grandpa sent at Christmas walked themselves to the compost pile while the moldy Monterey Jack made a mad dash for the trash.

Scott looked at the kids cowering in the corner then to the counter. On top of a paper towel where I'd scrawled, "Column In Progress: Do Not Disturb" rested my refrigerator treasures: my razor blade, dehydrated spinach, dog hair, rubber bands, a marble, sock, and plastic rectangle with the words, "Use one N battery".

"Honey," he said wrapping his arms around me. "You should've never opened that door."

To Clean Or Not To Clean?

I was picking strawberry filling out of the carpet in my minivan this morning. Normally, I'd leave these morsels for the dog's next ride, but tonight is my turn to drive the Bus Stop Mommies to Book Club. My van was its typical self – part trashcan, part Wal-Mart on wheels. One mom I know dubbed her minivan, "My Apartment."

Need a tissue? Got 'em. Baby wipes? Got 'em. At any given time, chances are good you'll also find jumper cables, bungee cords, air pump needles, Legos, gum wrappers, magazines, overdue library books, English riding helmets, folding chairs, golf balls, somebody's glasses, pencil stubs, loose change, dog hair, a tooth brush, petrified French fries, glass cleaner, compact discs (no cases), dirty laundry, year old receipts, rags, an AC/DC converter to a phone I no longer own, melted lip-balm, an outdated map, unmarked prescription drugs, used dental floss, Sharpie markers, Swiss Army Knife, nail clipper, gum wrappers, Happy Meal toys, a package that should have been mailed last Christmas, the complete Toilet In A Box kit waiting to be returned to Lowes, rain ponchos and umbrellas (but not when it's actually raining).

The good side is that the van is designed with seat back pockets and cubbies in which to cram stuff. Not only does that allow seating on the actual seats, but prevents potential hazards from unsecured items that would otherwise go airborne during a sudden stop. The bad side is that the van is designed with seat back pockets and cubbies in which to cram stuff. Entire colonies of life forms will be created and become extinct before I think to crawl in the third row of my van, hang upside down and reach into a space of which I can't see the bottom.

I was rejoicing in finding my favorite Tweezerman tweezers when it dawned on me. If I want to be a good friend and fellow mommy, I shouldn't be cleaning this van at all. Oh sure, it would be acceptable to wipe the snot off the seatbelts out of sheer courtesy, but not actually clean the whole vehicle. I mean, do I want to make my friends feel bad? Why, if they crawled into my immaculate van tonight knowing that their van sitting at home was one gummy bear away from a visit by the health department…that would be plain insensitive of me!

I gave up on the van and walked in the house. The house! What if they come inside before it's time to leave for Book Club? Should my kitchen counters be visible or can I leave out the recipes I've been organizing for the past three weeks? What about my prerequisite assortment of sacred piles? I could stash them in the oven and hope no one gets the urge to bake brownies.

I meant to have all these photos into albums by now. It's only been 7 months and my husband did say something about being able to eat at the table by Christmas.

The ring in the toilet has to go. That's just gross and I'm certain none of my friends ever let their bathrooms get to this point.

Oh, and what if someone wants to see the color I painted my son's room? (As if the swatch on the rear of my shorts wasn't enough of an indication.) I better clean his room, plus the two rooms and hallway we'd have to walk through to get there. I could take a chance that no one will look to the left when they enter the bedroom. That would mean seeing the kids' bathroom, complete with the remnants of the dog's bath and toothpaste art on the mirror.

"Hello Mindy? It's Karen. Listen, I'll just drive over and pick you up tonight. No really, it's not a problem. Trust me."

What's For Dinner?

I hate it when my kids figure out what my hot buttons are, then proceed to push them (and their luck) on a frequent basis. They think they're being funny too, which pushes another button. Inevitably some outsider (like Grandma) will laugh at their behavior and thus encourage them to do it again and again. I think I see the Parental Revenge Theory evolving here…

My kids are not stupid—they know the difference between intentional and accidental behavior. They learned from the Master—Me. They also know timing is essential. For instance, my daughter knows if she asks me "What's for dinner tonight?" anytime before say, 6 p.m., she should be prepared to run for her life to escape my wrath.

I want to be a dinner planner; it just hasn't become a habit yet… maybe it's because there are days when I don't manage lunch until 3 p.m. and am not hungry when the rest of the family is passing out from low blood sugar. Or maybe I'm so busy starting 18 household projects at once that I simply forget. Maybe after another fifteen years of married life dinner planning will become a routine, but I doubt it. By then, the kids should be gone and it's back to popcorn for dinner.

I realize there are plenty of you out there that know prior to sundown what your family will be eating for dinner. Some of you probably make a meal plan midday. You even have the main course defrosted and three side items to go with it. I bow before thee in extreme respect and total bewilderment.

Lucky for me, my husband is not a Mr. Meat and Potatoes kind of guy. I know real live men out there (who shall remain nameless so their wives don't suffer anymore than they currently do) who insist – insist I tell you – on every dinner consisting of a meat, potato and vegetable.

Those guys would be miserable in my house. A good day for me is having more than two colors on a dinner plate. This can include a bag of frozen broccoli and cauliflower. With a red meat, that makes three colors and I'm Julia Child.

Lest my mother read this column and call me to scream, "How embarrassing! You're going to make people think I didn't teach you how to keep a decent kitchen or cook a solid meal!" I should tell you that I really can cook. For years after the children were born though, it seemed pointless. Even after the baby food stage ended, it was senseless to make anything fancy, let alone a basic pot roast, just for the kids to wrinkle their noses and spit it out. At least the dog ate well during the toddler years.

During the early elementary school aged years, a balanced meal at our house consisted of macaroni and cheese with a side of peas. (See? Two colors. Three, if you include the parts of the noodle where the cheese didn't stick.) The meals were elevated to gourmet status when ketchup and ranch dressing appeared on the menu. Mary Poppins had a spoon full of sugar...I had a floor full of ketchup.

Now that my kids are older and willing to try a larger variety of foods ("Eat it or starve. See if I care.") I'm making an effort to actually plan a meal more than 15 minutes in advance. I'm using recipes a little more in-depth than "Add water and bake!" Sometimes the kids really surprise me with what they do and do not like. The entire time I slaved over Chicken Marsala (put it in the pan, take it out of the pan, put it back in the pan) I rehearsed Maternal Induced Guilt Speech #47: "After all I went through to fix this meal by gawd you are going to sit down and enjoy it... all the starving children in India... Don't tell me you're hungry an hour from now...."

No speech was needed; the kids loved it. They even gave unsolicited compliments and asked when we could have this fabulous dish again. I silently decided, not too soon, for fear it would become another run of the mill meal... "Oh no Mom, not Chicken Marsala againnnn!" The only family member unhappy that night was the dog, who for once had nothing left to lick off the plates.

I spent the rest of that evening awash in culinary euphoria until I went to tuck my sweet, well-fed daughter into bed. "Mom?"

"Yes, pumpkin girl?"

"What's for dinner tomorrow night?"

Cleaning Out The Pantry: School Supplies and Other Hazardous Materials

I was convinced the dog was eating the Monopoly Jr. money until I rummaged through the school supplies. Sure, I'd found some Fives and Ones stashed in the usual places—under the couch cushions, in the Barbie Uptown Girl folding townhouse, (so that's how the little hussy can afford her lifestyle), in overdue library books and the dryer lint trap.

Today I uncovered a two-dollar bill in the old Clementine citrus box labeled, 'Spare Notepads/Notepaper'. It was there in the pantry with the other clearly marked storage containers I was moving into the bathroom cabinets. Now that we joined a wholesale club, I need all the pantry space I can get.

I've gone to great lengths to provide a place for everything and everything in its place. My spasticity with organizing was born from 14 years of living in a 1300 square foot house. The mice had bigger pantries and closets than me. So what if my college girlfriends laughed at me because I made a grocery bag storage and dispensing unit out of an old milk jug? It worked great, saved space and cost nothing.

There's the old gift boxed set designed to house three VHS tapes. It's labeled, 'Tape and Glue' and holds an empty tape spool and six opened bottles of school glue. Naturally, I have no idea where the videos are that once belonged in said box.

Other containers, which in a former life resembled Tupperware circa 1972, are labeled, 'Red Pens', 'Sharpie Markers', 'Black and Blue Ball Point Pens', 'Pencils' and 'Misc.'. Everyone needs a 'Misc.' to cover school supply categories that are only pertinent every third year. Anybody need a protractor?

Two years ago, my son and daughter had to have their own personal tablet of composition paper. As in lined sheet music paper. They haven't needed it since. Then there's the graph paper of highly specified size, weight and proportion that we searched for throughout three states, finally ordering it off of e-bay. Apparently that kid never needed it either. I've yet to see a single graph come home.

I have every style, size and color of children's scissors ever made. Round tip, pointed tip, left handed, universal grip, shorter blade, longer blade, plastic blade, metal blade and every model called and priced like Fiskars. Each academic year a new style is requested and it's never the same as last year's. One year the teacher requested Fiskars brand but I defiantly sent my child to school with last year's generic model. After waking up for two weeks in a cold sweat fearing my child would be ostracized, I relented and forked over the extra few bucks for the name brand.

Pencils. If I had a nickel for every time my kids frantically dug through the junk drawer for a pencil two minutes after they should have walked out the door to the bus stop, I'd be, well, I'd have about $43.75. My son will use a pencil right down to the stub. I have no idea how he writes with that thing. The other day, while emptying pockets before doing laundry, I thought I hit pay dirt. Yum, a Good and Plenty. Then I bit into it and discovered it was, although a shade of its former self, a black pencil.

"Uh, son? Wouldn't you like a new, regulation length pencil to take to school today? We have 500 in the cabinet."

"Nah, that's OK. The eraser still works on this one." Gotta love the boy for saving us a buck.

My daughter is a different story. Not only does she prefer her pencils to have a child approved cool design on them ("Oh my gawd mom! Plain yellow?"), she 'needs' them ¾ length and above. So there in the deep dark depths of the box from my old Gypsy Jewelry Lovebead Kit, sit three dozen sparkly, seasonally emblazoned half used pencils.

I wonder if it would ruin his middle school career if I made my son use a stub with dancing snowmen on it....

Just Let Me Whine:
You'll Get Your Turn

I really was quite ill when I wrote this. I literally shuffled to the computer, wrote it, hit 'send' and shuffled back to bed. So if anyone's offended, blame it on the fever.

Sick Days For Mom?

Though I wouldn't trade Mommyhood for the world, I admit it has a couple down sides. One, a lack of annual pay increases. Two, no sick days. What's brought this to mind? The fact that I'm sitting here in my pajamas wanting nothing more than a new stomach and a one-way trip back to bed.

There've been times I've wanted to fake illnesses just to cop a day in bed in total denial of being a responsible adult…but this is real. Besides the obvious symptoms, I knew I was really sick when my husband knelt across the bed yesterday and said, "Wow, can I tell you how really bad you look?"

"That's right honey, I'm miserable…can you, whimper, get me some juice, ouch, and while you're at it, ow, help Melanie with her science project? And Morgan has a paper due tomorrow, gasp, Melanie has an orthodontist appointment Monday, heave, plus horseback riding lessons at Triple S. Call Carla to give her a ride…did Morgan do his homework? What about, wheeze, did you guys make it to church?"

There I am, in dire need of ibuprofen, a heating pad, six blankets and a stomach transplant and what comes out of my mouth? Wait. Bad choice of words. Try this: And what comes to mind? Concerns for the children and the smooth running of this household, not to mention their eternal salvation. I might be burning with fever but in my mind's eye I see next week's calendar perfectly clear. How sad is that? Do you think when dad is home (on a paid sick day) he is withering in pain worried about who has the next appointment or sporting event? Oh wait, bad choice of words again. I do know some dads that would rouse themselves from death to coach junior's next T-ball game.

However, most members of the male species who are ill enough to call in sick and get in bed, aren't worried about a thing. When they were younger, mommy pampered them and years later, many of them haven't changed. They're still waiting for mommy to bring them crushed ice, crackers and a comic book.

They expect that when they do rise from the great beyond of illness, their Fruit of the Looms will be clean and their socks picked up from the couch, laundered and matched.

And what will be awaiting us moms when we finally rise, usually way too soon, from our sick beds? Piles of dirty laundry, wet unidentifiables on the bathroom floor, dirty dishes all over what used to be the kitchen, take-out cartons in the living room, plus overflowing trash cans. At least you know the yard was cut because you heard the gas powered mower, edger, trimmer and blower just outside your bedroom window as you tried to sleep.

I've had wives tell me that if they're sick and want their kids to eat, they have to get out of bed to feed them. Can you believe that? We're talking honest to goodness high fevered barfing women here. I have two words for the husband who won't allow his wife Sick Days: LOOOOZ ZER.

"Geez, Karen! What am I supposed to do when my wife gets sick? I'm just a guy, after all, I can't help it!" Relax, it's simple. Escort her to bed, not the family room couch. Give her the remote control, juice, medicine, heating pad (the kids will know where it is) and extra pillows. Turn off the phone. Lower the blinds and leave. Take ALL children with you. Threaten them with no television or Christmas presents for the rest of their lives if they speak above a whisper or go within 10 feet of mom's door.

Feed the children (the cereal is in the pantry and the milk is in the fridge.) Clean the kitchen. Make sure the children make all appointments, games and social dates. If you're unsure of the schedule, check the calendar on the kitchen wall or ask the kids. Remaining questions get addressed to the mom next door. Whatever you do, don't ask your wife. Period. The only question you are allowed to kneel down and whisper to your wife on her Sick Day is this: "Is there anything else I can get you, dear?"

Women's Innate Abilities
(Or, The Top Ten Things That Won't Get Done Unless a Woman Does Them)

I was sitting at this computer, staring at the blank screen without the benefit of one full cup of coffee when I heard it. "Ahhh, what a beautiful sound." My mother looked at me in a worried fashion as she wiped spilled water with a paper towel. "What sound?"

"Of that paper towel ripping off the spool." I shimmied with delight, squared my shoulders, raised my eyebrows up and down and grinned.

She stared at me with that maternal, And Your Point? look. "Mom, the paper towel spool was empty yesterday and I didn't refill it. Normally, that wooden spool will sit empty for days until I fill it or make one of the kids do it."

"Karen, there are just some things that are innate to a woman's abilities and that, along with changing the toilet paper roll, is just one of them."

Well it didn't take much for us to get on a roll (I couldn't help myself) and rattle off 972 other abilities innate to women. For the sake of space and saving our marriages, we chiseled the list down to ten. Granted, it's not that the male or pediatric species can't do such tasks, it's just that, well, they don't.

Karen And Her Mom's Top Ten Things That Won't Get Done Unless Women Do Them:

10 Change out a bath towel. I bet I could walk into any man's bathroom at random and find a towel that's been in use since the Nixon administration. Naturally, wanting nothing more than our husband's complete comfort and well being, plus being less than fond of mildew laden stiff towels, the task of replacing his bath towel is ours.

9 Put away kitchen items. Emptying the dishwasher and leaving clean items on the counter doesn't count. After five years in the same kitchen, saying, "I didn't know where it went" is no longer a valid excuse.

8 Cleaning toothpaste spit off the bathroom mirrors. What are you people doing? Aiming the power toothbrush head directly at the mirror? Spitting

at your reflection? Down boy, down. Aim down.

7 Rinse toothpaste globs, shaved and tweezed hairs out of the bathroom sink.

6 Identify, let alone use, that thing in the corner of the bathroom behind the toilet. You know, it has a fairly long handle and rounded bristles on the bottom. Sometimes there is a plunger parked next to it. (Plunger they can relate to.)

5 Dusting. It simply never hits their radar screen. Nary a blip. Nada. Nothing.

4 Changing the sheets on the bed. What is it about men's total oblivion towards linens? To my husband's credit, he will make the bed and does so quite often. (I had to say that because he reads this column and even if he didn't, my kids would squeal.) However, changing the sheets ranks right up there with changing his bath towel.

3 Replacing the roll of paper towel. Pretending you don't know where I keep the extra rolls 'this week' is not a valid excuse.

2 Putting down the lid. Need I say more?

And the number one thing that won't get done unless a woman does it is:

1 Replacing toilet paper rolls. I walked into my children's bathroom the other day, something I try to avoid at all costs, and saw there was no toilet paper on the roll. The tissue box was empty.

I knew it'd been at least two full days since I'd been in there.
I didn't even want to think about it.

What's Wrong With This Picture?

My friend Racheal, God bless her, offered to take my children, along with hers, to the science museum downtown. Getting up, dressed and in functioning mode before 8:15 on a summer weekday was somewhat of a challenge, but well worth the effort when I thought of how quiet my house would be for most of the day. My husband's out of town for business, so it's just me, me, me.

And the dog. He doesn't talk back; ask me to make pancakes or stuff overdue library books under his bed. He did, unfortunately, pee on my bedroom carpet some time after I fell asleep last night. I know because it was already too dry to blot up this morning when I found it.

So today might be a good day to try out my new upright carpet cleaner whose box we've been walking around since I bought it on sale four weeks ago. I did tell myself I wanted to wait to use it until the kids were out of the house for hours on end…but was thinking more along the line of when school started. Then again, if I clean the carpets now, I'll have more time to put 10 years of photos into albums once school starts.

OK, so it's now 8:30 on a Friday morning and the dog and I are alone in the house. Wait. Make that the dog, me and my son's friend who spent the night. He didn't need to be awake and functioning for the trip downtown so there he sleeps, strewn across my favorite overstuffed armchair. Should I wake him up? Offer him breakfast? Treat him like my own son and order him put on fresh underwear and brush his teeth? I wonder if he'd just let himself out and ride his bike home if I crawled back into bed with my coffee, the remote control and newspaper.

Uh Oh, Domestic Guilt just hit. How could I crawl back into bed when I have so much to do around here? Maybe I should take advantage of the unseasonable low temperatures and start on all that yard work I've been putting off for cooler weather, like, November. After all, new neighbors just moved in behind us and I want to make a good impression before my kids get over there and make one for us.

The other day I let the dog out into the backyard and stumbled upon a troop of scouts hiking through with machetes. They were earning their Prehistoric Vegetation badge. I served them lemonade and asked them to keep an eye out for my birdbath. I hadn't seen it since I chipped the ice out of it in January.

Then again, I have been waiting for the perfect opportunity to clean out my daughter's room. This is an event that has to be strategically coordinated. First, said daughter must be out of the house. Check. Otherwise everything I chuck out of her room would find its way back within the half hour. Second, I must have an ample supply of large black plastic trash bags. Check. Third, I must wear hard-soled shoes to avoid serious injury from hair clips and Barbie doll accessories. Check. Fourth, there must be plenty of room in the giant trashcan outside to accommodate any such items that I find under her bed. Check. Finally, there must be no one else in the house so I am not overheard yelling obscenities or rhetorical questions such as, "What is that?" and "How long has this been under here?"

Hmmmmmm. So many choices, so little precious time alone in my own home. What's a girl to do? Ring Ring. "Hello Mel? It's Karen. What's up? Really? So are mine! Perfect. Meet you at the mall in an hour."

Now what to do with that sleeping kid?

My cousin, whose birthday is December 20th, asked me to send a copy of this to her mother.

The Christmas Baby

April 1964 was a very good year for some couples I know. Like my parents. And the parents of my friend Amy. And every other set of parents who were lucky enough to get pregnant in April 1964 or the month of April any year.

Unfortunately, their offspring weren't as lucky. We're the infamous December Birthday Babies. Some of us are known as the Christmas Babies, with birthdays that fall either on or within a few days of Christ's birthday. Six out of the sixteen women in my book club alone have December birthdays.

Catch me on a good day and ask, like folks usually do, "How do you like having a birthday three days before Christmas?"

"Well, as a child it was difficult. But now, my husband and kids make a big deal out of it so it's okay." On a bad day, "It stinks, thank you very much."

"Oh but WHY?" they gush. "I think that would be so special!"

Special? Picture this. Your child's birthday is in April. I send my kid to your kid's party with a gift wrapped in Christmas paper. In April. You think those moms aren't going to talk? The gift is a Christmas tree ornament. Now the moms are definitely talking. The kid is crying. No one thinks anything special about my wrapping paper, my gift or me. Rule #1 for giving birthday gifts in December: Never use Christmas paper.

For a child, a Christmas birthday can be traumatizing. Just ask my therapist. It shapes how you view anybody's birthday, at any time of the year, for the rest of your life. Your birthday happens over Christmas break, so you don't get to take cupcakes to your classmates, wear the Birthday Crown or be line leader. If your parents can manage a party during the holiday hoopla, it will be small. All your friends have already left for Detroit to see Grandma.

The most well-meaning friends and relatives forget December birthdays. And even if they remember, they're out shopping, out of town and out of money.

Someone joked recently that he used to be an atheist, but there weren't

143

enough holidays. This holds true for a little kid with a December birthday – not enough holidays. You get all your gifts at one time during the year. That's it. Then, without fail (because you're a kid, remember) March, April, May and June roll around and there will be something you're just dying to have: a new toy, a bike, a set of Clairol brown fleece wrapped gentle steam hot rollers. What do your parents say when you ask? "That's for a special occasion. Like your birthday." Or "Remember that when you write your list for Santa." Eleven months between gift getting is an eternity for a child.

One of the perks of getting older was my calendar of holidays expanded. I started dating Scott and suddenly had Valentine's Day to celebrate. I got a watch that first year. I'd never gotten a watch before that wasn't in a promotional Christmas gift box.

I married in June and gained an anniversary to celebrate. My husband looked at our newlywed closet and commented, "I thought all women had a ton of clothes. My friends warned me I wouldn't get any space in this closet. What gives?"

"It's summer. I have no summer clothes because my birthday was in December. Wait until winter. We'll need to buy a dresser or two just for the sweaters."

After a couple years and a couple kids, I added Mother's Day to my calendar. On top of that, I justify doing something special for myself on my kid's birthdays too. I mean, who did all the hard work here? Did you ever stop to think about that? We get fat, tired, hemorrhoids, poked, prodded, exposed, stretched as wide as Wisconsin and who gets all the presents for the rest of their lives? Those lousy kids who only had to pop out and scream for the next 18 years. And who keeps them alive, healthy, supplied with cheerios, clean underwear and poster-board from one birthday to the next?

Excuse me for a minute. I need to wire flowers to my mom.

I actually received a few nice answers to my 'ad'. But Greg was still the best.

Wanted: Respectable Car Mechanic

How many women out there have had it with auto mechanics' questionable dealings and treating us like dolts merely because of our chromosomal makeup? This column is for you and in grateful memory of Greg George. Maybe it's true that only the good die young. Greg was 39.

An ASE certified Master Auto Mechanic; he was dedicated to his vocation and customers, treating everyone with honesty and respect. I lost count how many times Greg rescued me from across town and drove me home. He'd fix my car and deliver it to my driveway—even if it was 10 p.m. Sunday. A father of four, he knew a reliable car equaled my sense of security.

I've yet to find another mechanic as remotely honest, competent and kind. The young man who fixed my flat at BJ's was an exception, but what happens when I need work beyond tires?

I tried a quickie oil change joint. The first couple visits were OK. I handed them my car, coupon and spent ten minutes with a bad magazine. The third time was the last. The guy noted it was over the mythical 3000 miles since I'd been there. He barked insults as if I was a child who just kicked his puppy. I wanted to kick him.

Earlier this month my brake light went on. I figured it was just low fluid, but since I was leaving on a trip the next day, took it into a shop for a looksee. The service writer had 'I'm on commission' tattooed on his forehead.

"Need the oil changed?"

"No, I had it done after Christmas."

"But it's been two months!"

"Uhh, right. I've at least two months to go based on the type of driving I do. I already checked the sticker. It confirmed when the oil was changed."

"Oh no! That sticker tells you when it's DUE for a change, not WHEN it was changed." I tried to explain that my dad filled out the sticker and did things differently; but the guy kept interrupting with his condescending lecture, not letting me finish a sentence.

145

Hours later he called to say it was just the brake fluid. Then tried his best to use my genetic makeup and pending road trip to scare me into $300 of additional work. I told him such maintenance wasn't due yet. He told me I was wrong and my owner's manual was lying. "Oh they write that but that's not really true."

It was too late to tell this guy not to touch my car. I was out $35 for degrading treatment and two ounces of brake fluid. I cut up my customer bar-code card from that place and wrote this classifieds ad.

Wanted: Honest, respectful car mechanic. Must work on my car as if his wife and children rode in it. Treating me like I'm stupid not necessary. I can get that at home for free.

Retailers Target Housewives

Give me free chocolate and shoulder harnesses in your shopping carts to keep my kid from jumping out and leave my frozen chicken breasts alone. We've got enough to think about as we're cruising the aisles without having to figure out which game the retailers are playing this week with our over-crowded heads.

How stupid do they think we are? 'They' being marketing gooroos at national retailers; 'we' being housewives. Why would I have an Herbal Essence Moment over the fact that the grocery store put their boneless skinless chicken breasts on sale this week? 'Buy one get one free, save at least $8.49 on two!' I might not be a calculus whiz, but I do know that yesterday, when chicken breasts were not on sale, they were only $5.99 a bag.

I picked up the Target flier Sunday morning and didn't know if I should laugh or gag. On the front page was a picture of a Calphalon cookware set. Underneath it read: 'This 8-pc. Cook-set – FIRST TIME under $100!'

The next line read, '99.99'

I'm supposed to get spastic over a penny? Don't these retailers realize that the modern women buying this cookware are college educated, number crunching, budget balancing, household managing, intelligent and savvy consumers?

I guess I shouldn't be surprised. Remember, this is a retailer that only has bathrooms in the front of the store, yet their toy departments are in the rear. Plus you have to wheel your kids past the snack bar popcorn machine to get to them. Mommy friendly?

Is anyone else out there really (and I mean, really) tired of being perceived as dense because you stay at home with your kids? Even June Cleaver would've seen that a set of pots and pans for $99.99 meant she'd have to ask Ward for well over an extra 100 bucks in the kitchen budget that week.

Then what about our fellow mommies who put in a full day's work outside the home only to put in another full day inside the home with dinner, laundry, the kids, homework, diapers, husbands, cleaning, budgeting and bedtime stories…it exhausts me just to think about it. These advertisements are aimed at them too.

So what's the message here from retailers? That they have to dumb down their marketing strategies to us simply because we've given birth? I know I've joked about delivering half my brain with the first child and the other half with the second, but God graces a mother's body with special ways of coping.

So what if I can't figure out what x equals if the leaf is 9 and the stem is 3 and Johnny lost 9 centimeters en route to Y. I can show my kids how to find the correct spelling of a word without using Spellcheck.

Just because I often open my mouth to speak and absolutely nothing coherent comes out, doesn't mean I need a job or a hobby. My husband still trusts me with running this household – including the finances.

Just because I can't always remember what day of the week it is doesn't mean I've totally lost all my intelligence. I still know a real bargain when I see one and who has the shortest lines at customer service.

So dear retailers, how 'bout cutting us some slack. And while you're at it, open some more check out lanes.

Communication

Still waiting for a local retailer to answer me. Can you imagine?

My Top Ten Questions For Local Retailers

One of the things I love about living in my town is that the stores I need for basic living are right here in town. I loathe dealing with Charlotte traffic, so the less I have to venture into 'the big city' the better. Since we're their biggest customers, the local retailers shouldn't mind a few affectionate questions from The Bus Stop Mommies.

Dear Local Retailers:

#10. Why do you bother building 30 checkout lanes but only open 3 at any given time? Please don't train your employees to roll their eyes at me when I politely ask them to open another lane. I'll simply return the look and ask another blue smocked employee the same question. By the way, I'm very good at rolling my eyes – ask my husband.

#9. Why ask, "Did you find everything OK today?" when you're ringing up my purchases. At this point it's, well, pointless. If I'm standing in the checkout line, chances are good I need to hightail it out of there a.s.a.p. to meet the school bus, make a doctor's appointment or save the dog from exploding on my new carpet. I don't have time to pause and say, "Well, now that you mention it, I did circle the store three times looking for prunes. Take me to them now. I'm sure the seventeen people in line behind me won't mind waiting a teensy weensy bit longer." You need to ask me, "Are you finding everything you need?" when I'm wandering aimlessly through the isles, mouth hanging open, emitting a funny whimpering noise.

#8. Why is it so dark in your store? Is it a proven fact that low lighting triggers spending? Or are you just trying to hide something? If you're thinking mood lighting, think swapping the fluorescent lights in the ladies' room for something more flattering.

#7. Speaking of restrooms – Will you please put restrooms at the front and rear of the store? It's a law of nature that a child will urgently need to 'go' once he's reached the most remote corner of the store. If your bathroom is up front by the food court, my child will start dancing in the garden shop. If your bathroom is back by layaway, he will grab his G.I. Joes when it's our turn in the check out line.

#6. If I am your 'Guest', why do I have to pay for stuff?

#5. How hard is it to keep those toilet seat cover dispensers filled? Or did I miss the Sunday Paper one week when Heloise described an alternative use for them?

#4. Don't you have spies who check out the competition? If so, why do you still charge twice the price for lettuce or a light switch than the other place?

#3. Do you ever test-drive your own shopping carts? Nothing can put me in a crankier mood than getting around the corner from the cart corral to realize I've picked a real clunker. Whappa whappa clunk clunk whappa whappa clunk clunk. The problem is not merely the buggy with the left front wheel that locks up and makes rude skidding sounds while we struggle to steer around corners…or wheels whose squeaks pop helium balloons and cause dogs in neighboring counties to howl in pain…oh, and the conjoined carts that land us on our rumps if we try to pull them apart. Here's the bigger problem: My kids, when small, got so used to wobbly carts that after awhile they found it soothing. So, when other parents swore by driving their colicky babies around in the car to lull them to sleep, we tried it too. Turns out this only worked for us after we let the air out of the left front tire of the Chevy.

#2. Must you continue to burden us with your silly promotions and ploys? I urge you, for shoppers with over flowing wallets, key chains and brains, get rid of those it's-only-a-bargain-if- you-have-our-store-card. Or perhaps we could just tattoo one universal barcode on the back of our hand and call it a day?

And the #1 question for local retailers is:

Why, when the average American woman (according to scientific surveys of my bedroom closet) is 5' 4" tall, do you stash stock on shelves 10 feet high? Please have your liability insurance premiums up to date so when I fall off the top shelf and get smothered by sugar substitutes, my family can hire a house-keeper, sitter and shopper. Finally, if you see size 5 ½ shoe prints on your shelves leading to the chocolate chip cookies, don't look at me.

This column was born after a night out with friends. The names and places really do exist and have not been changed to protect anybody. What am I, a reporter? After this column appeared in our local paper, I received very nice e-mails from the school principal and the mom of one of the prom goers who promised to give me photos from the evening. I'm still waiting.

Dear Parents of the J.M. Robinson High School Junior Class:

As a mother who will be in your shoes a mere four years from now, I grovel before you and beg you to pray for my children and me. Pray that on Junior Prom night, 2006, my son will be as charming as your sons were last week and that on Junior Prom night 2009, my daughter will be on the arm of an equally charming young man. However, I'd appreciate the caveat that she not develop a chest like your daughters' until her wedding night.

Let me explain (about seeing your kids, the chest thing should be obvious). Last Saturday my family went to dinner at our favorite restaurant, Tsunami. We met another family there, the Quinns. As we were waiting to be seated, in walked the most adorable group of prom goers, your children. The boys with their fresh shaven faces and stylish tuxes, the girls in their long feminine dresses and sparkly accessories. Smita and I sat drooling over their tiny waistlines, salon fresh hairstyles, smooth skin and white teeth.

We saw their teeth because they were all smiling, laughing and looking like they were truly enjoying themselves and each other's company. We were so happy for them…those fresh bubbly vessels of pristine youth who – "Mawwm, do you think the chef will let us play with his lighter?" – are not us.

Oh my gawd, are we that old? Did those Prom kids see us as a couple of chic and smart women who shop at the same stores they do, or as boring housewives who occasionally escape the tedium of cooking and cleaning up after dinner. I'm more than twice their age, but the funny thing is, I don't feel all that different on the inside. Do you?

It boggles my mind that I'm a responsible adult who gave birth to the twelve-year-old currently sitting at my kitchen table inhaling his third bowl of cereal. Who is he and how did he get into my home? And who was that Leggy Thing walking with her daddy up to the bus stop this morning with the long thick hair? The girl I gave birth to was bald and had a Buddha belly.

Back to dinner. We were fortunate to be seated at the same set of tables as our Prom friends. Smita and I snagged the birds eye view from the center of our table while Bob and Scott got to sit right next to your children and chat. Wow, look at that! Those handsome, young kids were actually conversing politely with our two old fart husbands. Prom Kid Parents—your years of hard work, nagging and sleepless nights are paying off! They even said Please and Thank You to the wait staff and clapped politely for the chef. We're really glad you taught them to relate to children. It was the highlight of the evening for our daughters when your sons came over and had their pictures taken with three little prom-dates-in-training.

I'd like to think that as I age, I can still relate to teenagers; that I'll always be one of the cool adults. I can see it now – Overheard in the halls of high schools all over the county: "Oh hey, you know that famous North Carolinian Columnist Karen Rinehart? Have you seen the way she dresses? I saw those pants at the Body Shop. Totally cool, dude. And that shirt – Gap! I heard she got her ears double pierced at Claire's. Have you seen the truck she drives? It's totally tight. I've seen her at the Clinique counter at Belk and see how she twists her hair up and fastens it with a pencil? The drafting teacher is mad cuz all his pencils are disappearing cuz all the girls want to copy her. Did she call you to baby sit her daughter? How phat is that?! Can I come with you? She has the best DVDs and even better junk food. She is sooooo cool."

In order to relate and maintain coolness with my own children as they grow older, I try to remember what it was like waaay back when I was that age: I'm nine and I'm stuck with a brother who is a freak and the dog is my only real friend; I'm ten and I stumbled over pronouncing a word out loud and started crying in front of the whole class; I'm twelve and all the other kids are still taller than me; I'm thirteen and I have ugly brown hair and no plans for the weekend. Ouch. It really doesn't seem that long ago after all.

Well my dear Parents of the J. M. Robinson Junior Class, I must go meet the school bus now; remember those days? Please tell your children how much we enjoyed their company and that we'd be honored to join them at their Senior Prom dinner next year.

Love, Karen

The Christmas Letter

"Hello my name is Kiki Rinehart and I'm a Self Serving Christmas Letter Writer." And so began my first meeting of Christmas Letter Writers Anonymous. The twelve-step program has been a godsend to me. I only wish I'd discovered it before I wrote this year's letter. As part of my program, I'm required to make amends to all those I have offended via my letter writing disease. I am also required to humble myself by sharing my most offending letter. So here it is, The Rinehart Christmas Letter, 2002.

Dear Family, Friends, Former Family members, and Former Friends I want to make sorry for choosing to no longer be our friends—

Wow! This year has really flown by! I know, because I've been tracking it on my lovely diamond studded, 20 karat gold Rolex. One cold day last February, I called Scott at work to mention I broke a nail. Being the thoughtful man that he is, he rushed home with the Rolex! It's certainly easier getting through an evening of giving Cook orders with such a thoughtful husband by my side.

March saw the loss of a treasured family member. We are all still in grief counseling over this. At $150 an hour, three hours a week each, our therapist is a miracle worker. After all, Ivana recommend him, so he must be good. Anyhow, we are comforted in knowing Biffy has the best hand carved imported Italian marble tombstone any hamster could want.

April showers may bring May flowers, but for us it brought a leak in the roof of our little home improvement project. No worries, Derek, our construction manager said Pierre can order new fabric for the seats that were dampened in the home theatre. Naturally, the little leak didn't hurt the natatorium and with the ongoing water restrictions, it's nice to get a few free gallons added to the pool and spa.

Gardener wasn't the happiest camper in May when we decided to host little Johnny's birthday party outdoors. Who knew those ponies made such a mess? Anyhow, it was a lovely day and as a party favor, all the children got to take home a saddle blanket for their ponies. What we'll do for Johnny's third birthday is beyond me!

Scottiepoo and I celebrated our wedding anniversary with a little cruise to Europe. It's amazing what they put into a ship these days! Did you know that the more cabins you book the better price you get? It's true. Just ask my cook, hairstylist, masseuse, nanny and laundress. Mummy and Daddy were so enamored with the bathroom fixtures in their cabin they bought the ship.

Whew, July and August were stifling hot. At least that's what the staff told us when we checked in from the Hamptons. A lovely breeze blew just for us all summer. Little Buffy enjoyed her first yachting lessons while Junior and Johnny practiced putting on the back yard greens.

Nothing says Labor Day like a BBQ in Kennebunkport. I must say, I've never seen Laura looking happier. Babs and I rekindled our long-standing Scrabble championship. I should learn the proper etiquette for letting the President win.

I trust you all received the e-photos from Halloween. As usual, Buffy and Junior won the Best Costume Awards at W.S.T.Y. Academy for Over Achievers. Vera stayed up until 3 a.m. sewing and suffered 3rd degree burns from the glue gun; but it was worth it to see the look on the faces of the store bought costume contestants!

November saw the Academy Homecoming come and go. It's always a joy to reunite with old classmates to catch up, trade business cards from plastic surgeons and confirm that our kids are smarter and cuter than theirs. Once again, Junior was chosen by his class to be Homecoming King, B.M.O.C. and Most Likely Not To Bankrupt The Family Business Upon Inheritance.

And here we are….December again! Where does the time go? Oh wait, let me check my Rolex!! Scottiepoo and I are humbled that our children's lists for Santa are selfless and scant – world peace, no more pesky neighborhood cats pooping in our flowerbeds and that every NFL franchise daddy buys this year will have a winning season.

We trust this letter will find each and every one of you wishing you were us. Do come see us if your travels bring you this way. The guest chateau is always open and the rates have never been cheaper.

God Bless Us Everyone,

Kiki, Scottiepoo, Junior, Buffy and Johnny.

P.S. You may be wondering what happened in January. That makes two of us! Needless to say the New Year's Party in Monaco was smashing!

My Funny Valentine (E-Mail)

Today I want to share with you an actual letter I received, via e-mail, from Loreal Cosmetics. My comments are in parenthesis.

Hello Karen,

It's Valentine's Day and the two of you are out for a late dinner. (Only because he was late getting home from work. Again.) Right after you're seated, the waiter reaches down and lights the candle at your table, setting your face aglow in soft, warm light. (Good. I need all the help I can get.) You see your Valentine's eyes sparkle. What's he looking at? Of course: He's looking at you. (No, he's looking at the prices. The sparkle is from tears.)Now that you've caught his eye, (and kicked him under the table so he'll stop commenting on the prices) you can use your natural instincts to your advantage. (I hope I have some left.) Here's three ways to do just that.

You look great tonight. (Why, thank you.) And so does he (Naturally. I dressed him.) – and you're showing that you notice. ("My new iron does a good job, doesn't it honey?") When you're attracted to someone, you often subconsciously bite or lick your lips, which can, of course, wreak havoc on your manicured look. (First, I only manicure my nails. Second, I'm biting my lip to avoid talking home repairs and dental bills on a rare night out.)You've got options. (You mean like, paper or plastic?) You could excuse yourself from the table and duck to the ladies' room for a quick reapply. (A good excuse to check on the kids.) And then do it again. (No way, the bread just arrived.) And again. (The wine was kicking in anyhow.) And again. (Get real.) Then, before you know it, you've spent more time in front of the mirror than with your Valentine. (And your point?)We suggest you instead choose a lipcolour (love the fancy spelling) that simply stays put. Lucky for you, L'Oréal Endless Lipcolour does just that. (If only my car keys followed suit.) Combining comfort wear, moisturizing power, and an eight-hour endurance, it'll ensure you look your very best on your special night. (I swear I just saw a flash of light bounce from Wonder Woman's 24-karat gold bustier.) And let you stay at the table so he can take it all in. (My good looks and not the bread, right?) You probably won't be able to tell, but your attraction to him will cause your blinking to increase. (My eyes always twitch when I'm tired.) Now's the time to take advantage of the extra attention you're drawing to your eyes. (Only if they hypnotize him: fix the icemaker…fix the icemaker…) Create an unforgettable look with L'Oréal Lash Architect: It's specially formulated to dramatically volumize, lengthen, and curl your lashes. (Does it fold laundry too?) All that, and it's designed to stay on all day…and night. (I'm sure the baby will notice at 3 a.m.) He'll simply lose himself in your gaze. Let him. (Hack, snarf, cajole, giggle, snort.)

Dinner's over, you look across the table and see that he's blushing, another sign of attraction. (His face is red because I just told him about that little parking lot /shopping cart/minivan mishap.) You smile, (without lipstick) blink once, (mascara in my eye) and ask him if he's…perhaps…interested in dessert? (Would never happen. We're dieting.) He smiles back and calls for the waiter. (And the check.)

You can blush right back at your Valentine when you wear L'Oréal Blush Délice, a sheer, soft-powder blush infused with Vitamin C to make your cheeks glow, and his heart flutter. (Powdered blush to make his heart flutter? I can do one better than that. Fresh batteries for the TV controller.)

Survival Mode

If you have any better hiding places, please share them with me! I won't tell your kids.

Hiding From The Kids

Shhh. Don't tell anyone where I am. I'm hiding out in my laundry room with my laptop. I feel like I'm doing something slightly immoral or at least illegal…but it's just past the half way mark of summer vacation and I'm beginning to get desperate for privacy.

I tried hiding in the bathroom but the kids found me there. And walked right in. When I started locking the door, they started slipping under notes. I installed a weather strip across the bottom so even a sheet of paper no longer fit in the gap between door and floor.

That's when my children, with whom I used to be so pleased when they used creative problem solving, scrawled extremely urgent, can't wait until you get out of the bathroom questions like, "Is there anything to eat in this house?" or "Have you seen my shoes?" and "Why was he born first?" on last year's poster board projects. They taped them on to my garden stakes, put on protective clothing and crawled through the prickly holly hedge under my bathroom window. Suddenly it got dark in the bathroom; was it supposed to rain today? I looked up expecting storm clouds and saw a bobbing picket sign, "The dog barfed on the new carpet."

Ha! I just heard my daughter tell my son that I'm taking a shower. I figured they'd stay clear of any room that held potential chores. I wonder how long I can pull this off. So far I've been in here longer than the bathroom and my most recent failed hiding place, the garden.

I made sure the kids understood that gardening was hard, sweaty, dirty, unpaid labor and for a while it worked. I enjoyed quiet morning interludes marveling at the flowers on my tomato plants. Then they got hungry, peeled their cute little butts off the couch and came outside to find me. "What's for lunch?"

"It's 9am."

"So?"

"Here, have a pole bean."

"Yeah right Mom. What can I really eat?"

"A pole bean. Would you like a broccoli leaf with that?"

"Mawwwwwmm!"

My next attempted hiding place was the attic. It's big enough to stand in, has lighting and averages about 113 degrees during the summer. I figured I could put on my bathing suit, grab a towel and a couple cucumber slices and pretend I was at the Bellagio Spa in Las Vegas.

As I lay there dreaming of a fruit smoothie and a masseuse named Sven, I heard muffled thumping and crashing noises from below. Then came the tapping on the living room ceiling. "Keep tapping, sis. When the tone changes from hollow thud to muffled thud, you know you found her. I've seen mom test for wall studs this way when she hangs pictures." At least this time I wasn't too disappointed in being found – the cucumbers dehydrated; the sweat stung my eyes and I think I had a splinter in my rear.

My friend Beth asked why I didn't hide in my closet. Last summer she stayed hidden two days before the kids found her. Her closet was so big it needed a fluorescent light fixture. She put her desk and computer in there and made it her home office. Mine is not so grand but after shoving some shoes and Christmas wrap out of the way, definitely big enough to sit in. Although not air conditioned, it's not as hot as the attic.

I told Beth I'd run in there now if I could find a flashlight that worked in this house. My closet has this normally handy feature where the light goes on when you open the door and goes off when you shut it. I don't know how to circumvent it. Otherwise I'd move a coffee maker, wine cooler and stack of magazines into my closet and never come out. Wait. That won't work. The kids could follow the trail of the extension cord.

Rats. The phone just rang and my daughter found me. I have to take this call; it's my mother—who would gladly tell the children where to look for me. Note to self: Put lock on laundry room door. Better yet, add electrical outlets and phone jack to closet.

End of Summer Prayer

I knew this day would come. It was just a matter of when and how bad it would hit. No, not another terrorist attack. I'm talking about the day when every mother sets down the dishrag, grabs her pounding head and declares to no one in particular, "Why on earth did I ever complain that summer vacation was too short this year?"

Oh sure we put on a brave face out in public. We participate in the standard prerequisite poolside conversation: "Mom #1: How's your summer going?" Mom #2: "Oh great, except there just doesn't seem to be enough time to get everything in...between trips to the lake, beach, camp, swim team, soccer practice, family reunions...summer break is just not long enough this year!" Mom #1: "Oh I know! Can you believe there are only a couple weeks left? Who at the school board had the harebrained idea to have such a short summer? I mean, there's no time to really do anything!" Every mother eavesdropping within a six-lounge chair radius has already had this conversation at least three times this month. In public.

In private, they have worn a path in the carpet to most remote corner of their bedroom where they sit for countless hours in a semi fetal position, rocking back and forth and humming off key. In private, these war torn moms utter prayers of desperation to a God who surely will give them the grace not to beat the precious gifts He bestowed upon them (when they asked) all those years ago. The End Of Summer Prayers go something like this:

"Dear God, Please get me through the rest of summer vacation. And God, it would be nice if you got me through it with all my hair still attached to my head, as I've noticed a lot of it is landing on my bathroom floor these days. I'm also seeing more gray hairs since May and the summer sun wreaks havoc on my roots. Oh Lord, help me believe "I'm worth it" and lead me not into temptation but past Miss Clairol to the higher priced Loreal boxes, even though my younger kids are hanging off the shopping cart head first and my older ones are lost somewhere in the electronics department.

While you're at it, please bestow upon Doug, the pharmacist, who has on more than one occasion incurred my lack of sleep wrath and bad hair day blues, enough Prozac in stock to get me through August. All my life Lord, the Church has taught me that you are a kind and merciful God. Well I could really use some mercy now as I head for the school supplies section. You see God, we have very specific lists of required supplies and my children have very specific tastes in three ring zippered binder fashions. The two will undoubtedly clash. And God, if it's not too much to ask, please let the 8th grade supply list arrive before orientation. Please don't take offense, but no amount of mercy or divine intervention could make me go to Wal-Mart the day before school starts for 13 different colored two pocket binders with metal tabs and a varied assortment of dry erase markers, highlighters and zippered pencil cases. I'll make my own pocket folders out of old Coke cartons and paper clips before I do anything that suicidal.

All school shopping aside Lord, I know we're in desperate need of rain, but please let the sun shine at least a couple hours a day until school starts so I can get my kids out of the house and into the pool. Then they can burn off all that excess energy from the Jolt soda and ice cream I caved in and bought them. Speaking of ice cream, if it's not too vengeful of me to ask, can you give the ice cream truck a flat tire this weekend? If I hear that clinkity song one more time I think I might climb a tall tree and never come down.

Well Lord, I better go do some more laundry and I'm sure you have a few things on your plate too. I know I've asked for a lot, but I promise if you answer my prayers I will never try to pass off deli chicken for my Grandmother's secret recipe homemade version ever again. Amen."

This one's for Mary Ann.

Home Alone

Hear that? That's the sound of absolute, unfathomable and utter joy. What you hear is me, alone in my own house. That's right, for the next 30 hours I am completely and totally alone. Unless you count the dog, but he doesn't talk back, hog the remote control, touch the computer or eat the last brownie.

Scott took the kids skiing and conveniently, I don't ski! Oh sure, there was a time when I snapped my boots into my bindings and prayed my butt didn't miss the seat of the chair lift. That all ended the day said bindings didn't release and the nice men with the red crosses on their backs gave me a free ride down the mountain.

I'll take the silence of my house over the thrill of a snowy ski slope any day. It's the most beautiful sound I never heard. No stereo, no cartoons, no whining. I turned off the computer speakers so I won't even have to hear Homer Simpson shout, "The mail's here, wooooo!" With the kids gone, the phone is guaranteed not to ring and no one will knock on my door. Scott took his cell phone, so no after-hours calls from it, either.

A girlfriend, also deserted by her family for the great white north, suggested we go out for sushi and a movie. As much as I'd like to park myself at Tsunami's sushi bar, sip a Sake Martini and enjoy adult conversation…staying home sounds much more appealing.

I can go out with my girlfriends when my husband and kids are home. And isn't that what makes those outings extra enjoyable? Besides, I have a couple large projects looming overhead that are far more palatable if done while alone in the house.

First, I have no less than 26 piles of file folders, newspaper clippings, household papers and receipts scattered about. This requires serious brain energy for sorting, labeling and filing. I need the peace and quiet to hear me talk to myself as I figure out what to keep, shred and why I saved it in the first place.

Then, there's the all-important task of the master bathroom. This is the project my husband not so subtly suggested I make progress on while they're gone. I don't know what the big deal is. It's only been a year since we started stripping the wallpaper. All that's left to do is spackle, prime, paint and reinstall all the towel bars and decorations. Then again, climbing the extension ladder with a bucket of paint might be fun without someone below telling me what I'm doing wrong.

Maybe if he sees how productive I am when left alone for the weekend, my husband will take the kids away more often. Quick! Where's that paintbrush?

Summer Vacation Begins

I've complained to anyone who will listen that two months is a sad excuse for a summer vacation. Whatever happened to Labor Day? The entire month of August? 8 weeks is barely enough time to fit in one camp, a trip to Grandma's, a broken bone and some time at the pool before the debate begins over zippered vs. nonzippered three ring binders. Summer break is just too short.

Feel free to remind me I said that come July 20th when camp is over, the pool is boring, every movie has been rented, Grandma's busy, the cast is covered with signatures, I'm covered with gray and even the dog is tired of playing outside.

Then again, if today is any indication of how this summer break is going to be, I won't need any reminders.

This first day of Summer Vacation 2003 has been a watershed of rain, phone ringing, phone dialing ("beep beep beep beep beep"), door slamming, rain, dog barking, glass breaking, bacon frying and nonstop chatter. And it's only noon.

For Mother's Day I asked for a folding table to stuff in my bedroom so I can write back here in peace. Except the house isn't that big so I can hear everything the kids are doing. This is good when they're whispering into the phone where to meet cohorts once they sneak out of the house.

But then I'll hear loud crashes followed by a frantic, "Nothing broke!" followed by an ominous two-minute silence. Hearing nothing is bad too. I try to ignore it, telling myself that silence is what I'm used to, what I live for. But then the maternal instincts kick in and I bolt across the house in search of likely disaster.

I've got to get used to having the kids around. Weeks from now I'll be looking for all new summer hiding places, but for now I'm just trying to stop twitching. Twice a year I experience instantaneous nanoseconds of panic as I adjust to a whole new domestic routine—the first day of school and the first day of summer break.

When the kids go back to school in the fall, I have to accommodate all new school, bus, athletic and extracurricular activity schedules. Twitch! What time is it? Twitch! Did I pack their lunches? Twitch! Did we miss the bus?

Twitch! Why is it so quiet? Twitch! Were there tryouts today? Twitch! Was I supposed to send something in to class today? Twitch! They're home already?

Summer brings its own adjustments. Twitch! What do you mean, what's for dinner? Did we even have lunch today?" Twitch! Has the phone ringer always been that loud? Twitch! Have you seen your little sister? Twitch! Didn't I just go grocery shopping yesterday? Twitch! That's not the sunscreen you dope! That's my $37 dollar anti-wrinkle cream. Twitch! Is Daddy home yet?

Twitch! Mom? Sorry, there's no one here by that name.

When you read about the things that hit the fans of fellow Bus Stop Mommies while their husbands were out of town, you might think I made some of it up. Either that or I drank the entire week's supply of cooking sherry the first day my husband was gone. You'd be wrong on both counts. It's all true. Except for the cooking sherry part. It was Chardonnay.

The Husband-is-Away-on-a-Business-Trip Survival Manual

With my husband's travel schedule this year, I've tasted a piece of single parenthood and it ain't pretty. I'm tired I tell you… tired and desperate to run away. As wives, we know that our husband's business trips can be a blessing or a curse. This is particularly true when their business, like that tiny little racing industry in which my husband works, takes them away on weekends. On the up side, we can rent chick flicks, have sole possession of the remote control and cook a dinner with only one color. Like popcorn.

On the down side, it's the weekend. The kids are out of school, which means zero private, quiet time, pizza delivery takes longer, the malls are more crowded and the days seem endless. Furthermore, anything that could possibly hit the fan will do so when the husband is on a business trip.

The Bus Stop Mommies and I compiled this abbreviated list of some doo doo that's hit our fans over the past year while spousal units were away.

* Car breaks down
* Ceiling leaks. On the new carpet. It's not even raining.
* Power goes out. Kids freak out. We want out.
* Teacher calls home and begins conversation with, "I'm really sorry to have to call you but…."
* Kids get stomach flu all long weekend, barf much, sleep little, recover miraculously Sunday night 30 minutes prior to daddy's plane landing. Mom,

meanwhile, still wears the results of child's stomach flu when daddy walks in the door.
* His cell phone breaks, the hotel operator wants proof you're his wife and all e-mail is down.
* Dog runs away. Again. This time he's not wearing his identification tags.
* Record breaking freeze experienced. In May.
* School play, church program, soccer championships and best friend's birthday party all scheduled for same day with overlapping starting and ending times.
* Teacher calls again.
* Credit card is rejected at check out with cart full of milk, meat and special survival stash of chocolate.
* Husband's long distance phone calls always seem to correlate with the children's temper tantrums, diaper explosions, dinner (popcorn) burning, doorbell ringing and dog running out of invisible fence zone.
* Mom gets stomach flu. Does not recover before daddy gets home. House shows it. He has no clean boxers for Monday morning, milk is sour and car keys are missing.

In between dodging the flying debris, we temporarily single moms shift into survival mode with a few lifestyle adjustments:

Dad is away on a business trip survival menu:
Breakfast: Sugar bomb cereal or toast
Lunch: Whatever the nice school cafeteria ladies feed them
Dinner: Anything eaten in front of the fireplace or TV. Preferably something I would not in a million years fix when dad was home, ie. sugar bomb cereal, toaster pastries, fish sticks and anything delivered. Did I mention sugar bomb cereal?

Weekend meals when dad is gone take on a slightly different flair.

Breakfast: Chocolate Chip pancakes to impress kid who spent the night
Lunch: Hot dogs from street vendor.
Dinner: Any place that takes VISA on the way home from Saturday evening Mass.

Dad is Away On A Business Trip Sleeping Arrangements:

Daughter and dog in my bed. Son stays in his room...unless it is the weekend, then he and another teenager crash, still clothed and with glasses on, before the warm glow of the TV screen. My sleep is guaranteed to be disrupted by daughter thrashing about and dog experiencing whimpering, whining, twitching nightmare. Dog will also wake to bark at cats fighting next door.

Dad Is Away On A Business Trip Reunion Tips:

Throw the kids at daddy as soon as he walks in the door and go hide in the bathroom. Feign illness if you must. You know you'll just start fighting if you speak to each other the first hour he's back...so take advantage of the adjustment period and take a bath.

Oh great. My husband just informed me he must fly to Delaware this weekend. "Grab the dog, kids. We're going to Grandma's."

Quirks, Hobbies, Traditions

I can't believe Cosmo hasn't called and begged me to be on their cover.

Confessions Of A Magazine Freak

I'm a magazine freak. The older I've gotten the worse my desire has become. Maybe because they meet the needs of my aging, ever occupied brain. It's what I like to call Short Attention Span Theatre Reading. You know, short meaningless articles easily digested during a bowl of cereal or Trading Spaces commercial break.

One of my favorite magazines is *People*. The letters to the editor are amusing and the captions are top notch. Captions under pictures are a necessity when you're pressed for time. With them, you get the basic who was there, with whom and what they wore. This comes in handy when your orthodontist can rewire your kid's braces faster than you can read the entire story on yet another Hollywood wedding under a big white tent on some exclusive ranch with helicopters swooping low despite secrecy from the paparazzi.

Magazine devotees like me face a few quandaries. First, finding space to keep them. Second, they can be downright expensive. When the grocery budget makes us choose between a month's supply of wrinkle cream or glossy pages, well, it's tough. Finally, and probably one of the least considered downsides of loving magazines, is hiding them from the kids.

"Hey Mommy, what's menstrual relief?" is not something I necessarily want to discuss at this point and time in my child's life. Even advertisements and articles in a seemingly harmless fitness magazine can open the door to real humdingers.

I got excited recently when my husband brought home magazines from his office recycling bin. It didn't matter that the *In Style* was a year old or that *People* was from last week. We had a road trip ahead of us and I was amply armed without spending a dime.

What I wasn't armed for was the copy of *Cosmopolitan* included in the

175

stash. Which rhymes with Trash, which describes any issue of *Cosmo*. Call me a prude, but I never was, nor will I ever be, anything remotely related to a Cosmo Girl. I actually got embarrassed reading that magazine.

Even if you take all the X- rated articles and ads out of it, it's still full of shallow fluff that as a housewife and mother, I just don't have time to worry about:

"Score Scented Strands!"

"4 Tress Traumas Solved!"

"Can a Serial Dumper Ever Settle Down?"

"I Keep Reminding Myself That Michelle Pfeiffer Was Once a Checkout Girl."

"White Looks Good Against Your Skin, So Show a Little...or a Lot!"

If by "dumper" they mean a non-potty-trained toddler...and if the white that "looks good against your skin" is a burp cloth, fine. But you'd still be better off buying the wrinkle cream instead.

Horseback Riding Lessons

As we were brushing down our horses this morning, my classmate Amy asked, "When are you going to write about taking riding lessons?"

"Uhh, when I can think of something to say about it that's not totally embarrassing? Besides, who other than my orthopedist and insurance provider would be interested in my new hobby?"

"Oh come on now, Karen. Who can't use a good laugh these days?"

I don't know...it was scary enough to actually pencil my name on the lesson schedule after 12 months of saying I was going to; now I'm supposed to talk about it? I hadn't embarked on an adventure of this magnitude in over eight years (please don't ask about the golfing experiment, it's still too painful). A middle aged woman's ego is endangered enough without throwing something new and different at it that's not chocolate or edible.

Look at what I put myself up against: There's the horse—a young, spry, four legged, gazillion pound, eight-foot tall creature. Then there's me—a middle aged, two legged, crackly kneed, 100-pound weakling. I can barely reach over the horse's ears to put on the bridle and the stuff I have to pick out of their hooves smells worse than a diaper after strained liver.

To make matters worse, my daughter had been riding a year and a half and has become quite accomplished. I was risking the very cornerstone on which we as parents base our authority...an existence of knowledge, skill and experience for our children to emulate and dream of achieving...translated: My ten-year-old was going to know more about something (a heck of a lot more) than me. "Yeah Mom, heh heh, I can't wait until I have a day off from school so I can come watch your lesson!"

Not only does this venture of mine require new athletic skills and three tubes of Ben Gay after every ride, it requires a whole new vocabulary. The tables have turned and now my daughter can quiz me every week. "No Mom. That's not a 'strap'. It's a 'girth'. Now I want you to write it 25 times until you get it right. What? NO! We don't say 'giddyup'. Really now Mom, if you're going to embarrass me like this, I'm just going to leave you home next time. Now tell me the difference between a halter and bridle...."

Years ago I went through my tennis lessons stage. I wanted to blend with the other suburban moms at the grocery store with my swingy little pleated skirts and anklet tan lines. Translated, I was in it for the clothes. This is certainly not the case now. Riding breeches must be the most unflattering sports attire ever created. Ladies' golf attire is typically an embarrassment to our breed; but at least the panty lines are avoidable. After two lessons in blue jeans and bruises on the inside of my knees the same color, I came to terms with the breeches. After six weeks of lessons, I finally found a style of underwear whose panty lines don't make it look I have three separate rear ends.

Michael, my instructor, warned me as I slid off the horse after my first lesson that I'd have "spaghetti legs" for a while. In all my newfound bravado (from actually staying on the horse the full thirty minutes) I thought, *What is he talking about? Surely that won't apply to me. Why, I walk to the bus stop twice a day without losing my breath. I walk up and down the aisles of the grocery store two days a week. And let's not forget about the mailbox—it's all the way at the curb!*

I put away the saddle, brushed the horse, then puttered around the barn for a bit before I sauntered my Scarlet O'Hara self to the van. For the love of God I couldn't lift my foot from the brake to the gas pedal. I flipped on the windshield wipers thinking it was drizzling before I realized it was just me crying. Miraculously I made it home and into a hot shower. I'd have taken a bath, but couldn't lift my legs over the side of the tub.

The next morning, I knew why all those actors playing cowboys walked like they still had a horse between their legs. There wasn't a spot on my body that didn't hurt, but my legs took the prize. Even Suzanne Sommers' thighs couldn't conceive what I was feeling. I whimpered and limped my way toward the bus stop. After five minutes, I'd made it to the middle of the driveway. "Come on Mom, hurry up! I'll be late."

"Go, ouch, on without me ow I'll oh my gawd catch up. Better yet, go get your father so he can carry me back into the house. I don't want the neighbors to see me like this."

A week later my next lesson rolled around. By then I could get out of bed in the morning without crying, but seriously questioned why I was doing this to myself. I reviewed all my plausible excuses: this would be a great mother daughter bonding experience; I could better understand how difficult her lessons are; it's an excuse to buy new clothes and accessories. Besides, with all this pain, it must mean my thigh muscles will be back to their pre-pregnancy shape by Christmas, right?

I said, right?

Receipt Junkies

In my billfold, I have more receipts than money. But in my house, receipts can be more valuable. Today, if my search yields the right receipts, it's worth $150 in vision insurance reimbursement. My billfold has never and will never see the likes of that in actual green stuff.

My husband uses Microsoft Money on our computer to track income, expenditures, bill schedules, short and long term budgeting. We're also trying to figure out where all the money is going so quickly these days…hence the receipts. And not that I'd ever forget to record the amount of a check in the ledger, heh heh. (Did you see that episode of Life With Bonnie?)

Fortunately, my husband is not as detailed in his data entry as he used to be. In the past, I was required to turn in a receipt for every single teensy weenie purchase.

Do you know how awkward it is to ask a soda vending machine for a receipt? And how about the times I caved in and got the kids a gumball out of the machine at the barbershop? Where do you get a receipt for that? "Kids, go pick a piece of paper out of that trash can, blow off the hair and write down, '3 cents, bubblegum'. Give it to daddy when we get home."

All expenditures were broken into categories – food, drugstore, entertainment, school expenses, medical, lawn and garden, dog, utility bills, travel, etc. I'd write across the top of the receipt which category it fell into. This got tricky. Is a candy bar "groceries"? If I bought it at the drugstore did that make it a toiletry? If it's for PMS, is it a medical expense? I finally entered it under "entertainment."

I don't know why he bothered to include an entertainment category for us; the kids were the only ones having fun.

I don't know why he made a "Karen" category either. It was depressing. Not only was there zero contributed from me under "Income," I made the most expenditures. I started to look very irresponsible and greedy until it dawned on me. This is my job. My husband makes money; I spend it. I do all the errand running, medical appointments and shopping for the household and the family, so who else's name would be on all those receipts, the dog's?

Speaking of the dog, twice a year when he enters the vet bill into the computer, my husband sits Hank down and gives him The Talk. "Do you know how lucky you are? Do you know how much you cost me? Next time you decide to run away you just keep running because I'm not taking you back. Next time you feel like peeing on the new carpet, just remember who rescued you and show your gratitude. Another day at that pound and it would have been lights out for you ol' boy. Now go play and for Pete's sake stay healthy."

Obviously written before the National Do Not Call Registry was formed!

Toying With Telemarketers

"Hey Mom, why don't you write a column on telemarketers?"

"Good idea honey," I muttered as I walked back and forth through the house forgetting why I was going that direction in the first place. "I will."

"Will it be in the paper this Saturday?"

"Uh, um…" I attempted to sort through three days worth of mail so I could use the kitchen counter again. "I, uh, well no son. Don't you have homework?" I was having one of those I'm Totally Overwhelmed Weeks where everything happens in a span of four days after you've sat bored for the last twelve.

Between Monday and Thursday, there were kids' horse lessons, school orientation, orthodontist appointments, Bible study, my riding lessons, post riding massage, book club, dentist appointment, packages to mail, gifts to buy, a date to pick out color swatches with a friend and two lunch dates. Add to this writing two weeks of columns in half the time so I could leave for Arizona on Friday morning. I started twitching just thinking about it all.

I was sitting at the computer reminiscing of more mysterious items found in my kids' backpacks when the phone rang. The Caller ID displayed, "Unknown Caller." Typically, we ignore these calls because if you spell "Unknown Caller" backwards you get, "Telemarketer."

However, the other number that shows up as "Unknown" is my husband's office number. Being the gem that he is, Scott calls about this time each day to say he's on his way home and ask if we need anything.

At great risk to my sanity, I answered the phone. "Hello! Is Scottm there?" I tried not to laugh at the poor girl, she was so serious. "No (giggle) you have the wrong number."

"Oh, um, is it just Scott? Is Scott there?"

"No, you still have the wrong number."

"It's the wrong number?" I crossed my eyes until the wallpaper blurred.

What part of wrong number did she not understand? "Yes dear, goodbye now."

About a million years ago, Scott's name was printed as "Scottm" on his Delta Frequent Flyer program materials. Subsequently, we have received approximately 923 pieces of junk mail, both in Florida and North Carolina, addressed to Scottm M. Rinehart, Scottm Rinehart and Mr. Scottm. A few have been addressed to my alter ego, Mrs. Karen Scottm. This was, surprisingly, the first time a telephone telemarketer had ever used the name.

In Florida, for 5 bucks a year, the Department of Agriculture would put your name and number on a "No Solicitations" list. Anyone who did not cease and desist calling would get one warning from the state, then after the second incident, slapped with a felony charge plus fines. It was a beautiful thing.

Outside of a few charitable organizations and parental units, we received nary an unwanted call. Since we moved to North Carolina, I've had to refine my tact with solicitous phone calls. To add insult to injury, the callers ask for not only us, but also the last person with this number. (Tina Hill, if you're out there, the salesman at the Honda dealership is looking for you.)

At first I remained calm by repeating this mantra to myself: "At least they're working for a living." I'd say, "No thank you. Please take our name off your list. Goodbye." After one particularly stressful domestic day, the phone rang. Thinking it was Scott, I answered.

"Hello! Is Karen Rinehart there?" Without hesitation I answered, "No. She died."

"Oh, uh, oh, I am SO sorry!"

"Thank you for your sympathy. Please take her name off your list."

Click.

I Love My Sleep

The best bumper sticker I've ever seen in my life read, "I have absolutely no idea what I am doing out of bed." Now here I sit on a Monday morning wondering why I'm even awake and functioning in the first place. Right, the workmen are scheduled to start today and seeing as how it wouldn't have been quite proper to leave a note on the door reading, "Let yourselves in. Make coffee before you wake me with the sound of power tools," I opted for being out of bed, dressed and armed with my two cup minimum of coffee.

That was two hours ago. I hate realizing I could have slept another hour. I was so tired this morning that even the dog hopping on the bed and sticking his tail in my face couldn't make me get out of bed. Oh sure, shift away and shove him over to my husband's side of the bed, yeah, but not actually get up and out.

That's what I get for staying up late and watching all those educational and entertaining shows on The Learning Channel. Being the bad mom that I am, I let my kids stay up and watch *The World's Most Dangerous Police Chases* with me. Who could resist? At this moment, as they were two hours ago, my children are snug in their cave like rooms – all dark and cool, the blinds closed tight and the soft purr and caressing breeze of the ceiling fans. All I want to do is crawl in bed with them. I'm thinking about going in and waking them up just to be spiteful, but why spoil the only quiet time this house will see all day? Is not my sanity worth more than well disciplined, highly productive, non-slothy kids?

Obviously it's summer and this type of slack behavior wouldn't happen during the school year. Really, it wouldn't. I swear. Oh all right, there've been occasions where, once the kids were loaded safely into their busses, I shuffled back into the house and onto the couch. Somehow, going back to sleep on the couch with Fox News in the background didn't seem as bad as crawling back into my actual bed. Besides, I always had a perfectly justifiable reason for needing more sleep – a cat fight woke me up in the middle of the night, I had the flu, I was out of creamer for my coffee, the dog had the flu, I was going to have a late night at PTA, some kid in China had the flu…you get the picture.

Granted, some days I'm a virtual Superwoman of productivity caught up in a flurry of washing, drying, folding, ironing, mopping, dusting, gardening, cooking and whipping up new living room curtains. Even Martha would stand in awe. Other times it's all I can do to make sure the kids have clean under-wear for the morning and something resembling bread to put in the toaster. Then I wish I was more like that one Bus Stop Mommy who consistently has an entire day's worth of domesticity accomplished by noon. The toilets are scrubbed, floors are clean, laundry is done, her kids have eaten breakfast and lunch, the grocery shopping is complete and dinner's in the crockpot. Good thing she's my friend otherwise I'd hate her.

I suppose I'd be content to find a happy medium somewhere between sloth and Superwoman. A place where there's always clean underwear in the kids' drawers but not necessarily their favorite "Princess" shirt. When the kitchen floor doesn't sparkle but my feet don't stick to it either. Where there's food in the pantry but it hasn't quite made it to the stovetop. When there aren't enough hours in the day to check everything off my To Do list, but always enough time to receive a kiss from my child. And just as impor-tant, when I can go to sleep and wake guilt-free knowing I'm doing the best I can. Yep, that's the happy medium I'm going to aim for.

After I take a nap.

The Fashion Maven That I Am

This is my parents' favorite column. Maybe that helps you understand me a little better.

Invisible Underwear?

Boxers or briefs. Guys, as usual, have it so easy. Not only do women have to choose between boxers and briefs (yes, gentlemen, there is the ladies' version of boxer shorts), we have to decide on low cut, high cut, bikini, hipster, body contouring, French cut, basic brief, boy cut brief, cotton, cotton blends, seamless, seamed and that nasty invention that today's teenage girls deem necessary to share with us out the back of their blue jeans, the thong.

As if those aren't enough choices, we have to micro manage our supply according to which type we wear for yard work, running, walking, white pants, blue jeans, low rise pants, waist huggers, tennis, Sundays, painting, fat days, thin days, clothes shopping and that elusive date with our husbands.

Even the difference in packaging is a world apart. I opened a new seven-pack ("Six Pair plus a Bonus 7th Brief!") of Fruit of The Looms and would you believe they were all tucked neatly inside one another? I mean, two stacks of nestled briefs crammed into a 3 ½ by 5 plastic baggie. How did they do that? It was a No Binding Cotton explosion in my laundry room when I opened them for the pre-wash.

Guys don't worry about panty lines either. I was cruising the lingerie department at Wal-Mart, waiting for my pictures to be developed, when a new product caught my eye:

"Hanes Her Way 'in·visi'ble' Underwear that disappears under your clothes". Where does it go? I was dying to know; so after a ten-minute debate on colors, I tossed a Blush/Beige combo in the cart. They were a bit pricey, but I had to squeeze into my riding breeches the next day and I was desperate.

This ladies' two-pack was the same price as the seven-pack of guy's FOTL's, with three times the amount of cardboard and hype. Fifteen flaps, tabs, slots and folds later, I opened the package and freed the panties, only to reveal intricate written and diagrammed packing instructions.

187

Was I supposed to refold and store my Invisible panties in the original package? Would they become Visible if I didn't? Would some government warranty be voided if I just threw them in my top drawer with the ordinary line-making panties?

In complete fascination, I stared – and I am not making this up – at steps A through G. I saved the package in case you don't believe me. I can barely believe it myself...and yet I quote:

"(A) Lay first garment face down on a table. Lay second garment face down on top of first, 1 ½ inches higher. Place unfolded package on top of garments with insert panel top edge even with top of second garment as shown. (B1) Fold bottoms of garments up. (B2) Tuck ends of garments under. (C) Fold right sides over. (D1) Fold left sides over. (D2) Pop up center flap. (E1) Fold garments and panel up. (E2) Place center flap over garments. (F) Fold left side flap over garments and (G) insert tab into back slot. Adjust garments as needed for proper display."

What I do know is that this was no ordinary underpaid immigrant or 8-year-old Chinese kid packing this underwear. The package says it was assembled in Honduras, yet the folding instructions were written only in English. Anyone wanna lay bets on where all the former Enron employees have gone?

Victoria's Secret

After years of squeezing a family of four into a budget built for two, I've learned to accept the necessity of smaller numbers on things, like bra sizes and price tags. So imagine my thrill when my mom gave me a gift certificate for Victoria's Secret.

It'd been countless years since I ventured into that store, and with the exception of angel wings everywhere, not much had changed. The music? Same. Décor and smell? Basically the same. The prices? More outrageous than ever.

One bra was almost $39. THIRTYNINE DOLLARS! That's more than my last water bill. And it didn't sing, dance, feed the dog or come with poster board for tomorrow's school project.

Another bra had some sort of gel or water filling. Now that one was a little tempting, but with my luck, I'd go out to dinner, get a little careless with my chopsticks and the thing would burst in the middle of a crowded dinner show at Tsunami.

They still hang stuff real high on the walls too. In one corner, up near the ceiling, big letters spelled out, "Wireless."

"They sell phones here now?"

"No, those are wireless bras."

"Where? I don't see any."

"Way up there. Keep looking. Up. Up. Stop right there. Those two small rows." My six-foot-one husband stood on his tiptoes, reached up, gave one a squeeze and said, "Hey, you're right. No wire. What else do you want to look at and should I see if they have extension ladders?"

We wandered around the underwear tables. So many choices, so little fabric. There were so many thongs I felt like I was in the sling shot isle of Outdoor World. Although none of the taxidermy animals on display there were wearing white-feathered angel wings or listening to classical music.

I found a pair that vaguely resembled the stuff I had in my drawer at home. I stood there thinking, *Would these leave panty lines under my sweatpants?* when my husband asked what size I wore. Forget it! (Even I'M not going there in this column.) But I'll tell you this; Victoria Secret's sizing is different from the chart on the back of a Hanes Her Way three-pack. Show me a woman that wears size "extra small" panties and I'll show you a woman that has some weird, rare allergy to desserts…poor thing.

I picked up pair after pair of fancy underwear, turned them over, looked at the tiny rear views and thought, *There is just no way*. Then I saw it—a sign from the underwear angels themselves: "Buy three pair for $19.95, get a free roll of heavy duty double sided tape to hold them on!"

Sold.

Housewives Set Modern Fashion Trends

This morning I logged onto Foxnews.com for my daily dose of intelligence (which seems to evaporate each night as I sleep). I skimmed the home page until a bright photo and headline caught my eye, **Pajamas Get Out of Bed**, By Amy C. Sims. Um, and your point? I mean, typically my pajamas get out of bed with me every morning. It's warmer that way and I don't make a habit of parading around naked in front of my children. Obviously this article commanded my further investigation.

"Pajamas are coming out from under the covers and into the streets, making daytime as cozy as nighttime." And this is *new* news? Even without the benefit of my third cup of coffee, it became brilliantly clear to me that Ms. Sims has never struggled to get children out the door in the morning. Hence, she has never had the pleasure of driving to school in her pajamas, praying it's not the day she gets pulled over for not making a complete four wheel stop at the blaring red sign.

Nor has poor Ms. Sims indulged in the luxurious housewife privilege of frequenting street corners in her pajamas without garnering weird stares from passersby. Translated, she has not hung out at the bus stop chatting with fellow moms in rubber soled slippers, plaid pj bottoms, fluffy robe, cup of coffee, yesterday's mascara and a ski hat.

"'Pajamas are definitely a style on the streets these days,' said Taina Medina, 21, a receptionist at Lucille Roberts gym in New York City. 'People shop for pajamas like going to buy a pair of Gucci pants. I iron them; they are like an outfit. And guys like the plaid pajama pants… like the old man sitting in the house look, just chilling.'"

I'm going to be gracious and take Miss Medina's youth into consideration when I tell you she is totally clueless. Number one, we housewives have been wearing our pajamas on the streets for generations now. Fearless stay-at-home moms are the true trendsetters of this fashion nation. We merely humor such publications as *Elle*, *Vogue* and *Cosmo*, letting them think they are the brink of fashion discoveries for the sake of the American economy.

Further, trying to compare shopping for pajama bottoms to purchasing a pair of Gucci pants is like trying to compare picking up a packet of Kool-Aid over a bottle of 1985 Chateau Cissac Pellation Haut-Medoc Controlee Cissac Gironde. Oh, and anyone who irons their pajama bottoms is just plain sick I tell you, sick. And dangerous. And in need of serious therapy.

"Medina loves the look and feel so much she was even wearing her PJs to work. But apparently her boss isn't so hip on the latest style. 'I can't wear them at work anymore though, 'cause it's not proper work attire,' she said."

Shocker! A receptionist at a swanky NYC health club is not allowed to wear her pajamas to work. What is this world coming to? Where are her rights? Where is the NOW gang? Where is New York Senator Hillary Hyphonated Clinton? The ACLU? Sue, sue, sue!

We housewives face no such constrictions. We have no boss telling us how to dress, let alone where and when to wear our plaid flannels. Yesiree, ours is the life of true freedom of expression envisioned by our founding fathers (whose wives I bet hung out at home in their PJs too). Speaking of freedom, our little fitness club friend Miss Medina chimes back in—

"'It's such a comfortable feeling, like a feeling that you're at home,' said Medina. 'Wearing you're pajamas outside is like showing you are free.' "

Alexandra Cohan, a Spokesperson for Old Navy Stores, concurs, adding "that wearing the soft, familiar pajamas can make people feel as secure and comfortable as being at home—even when they're outside: Comfy clothes make you feel safe. The types of clothes that you would traditionally wear at home, which is a safe place, can translate out to the streets."

The article goes on to quote Renee Claire, owner and designer of BedHead, (she stole that nickname from mothers of young children) a line of sleepwear sold in over 1,000 stores nationwide. Ms. Claire says. "The comfortable, loose drawstring or elastic-waist pants are especially popular." Now here's a woman that might have actually given birth if she recognizes the comfort in an adjustable waistline. Either that or she knows what it's like to wake up and attempt to get dressed the morning following a binge of late night cookies and beer during the latest Trading Spaces rerun.

So there you have it. If you want to be safe, wear your pajamas. If you want to be comfy and wear your pajamas while you work, become a house-wife. Want to feel safe and secure out in public during our heightened state of terrorism awareness? Wear your pajamas and / or become a housewife. Want to be traditional? Become a housewife and continue to wear your paja-mas long after the bus has left the stop (remember the non-binding waist).

Want to be original, chic, trendy, hip, comfy and cool? Wear pajamas all the time, everywhere, have kids, hang out at the bus stop, relish the freedom, innovation and luxury of the housewife life.

The Big Bang Theory, Bus Stop Mommy Style

"Hey Pam, your hair looks cute like that." Pam's weak "thanks" sounded more like an apology as she fiddled with her headband. "I'm letting my bangs grow out and this is the only way I can wear it these days." You'd have thought she announced her puppy died. Fourteen genuinely empathetic female heads turned towards Pam to offer condolences, encouragement, unsolicited advice and hair taming tips.

There were more shouts of "Hang in there!" "You can do it!" and "Don't let the idiots get to you!" than at the local little league game. What you couldn't hear or see were the bets being slipped under the table on how long it'd be before Pam gave up the good fight, locked herself in the bathroom with her kid's school scissors and hacked her hair back to the land of the living bangs.

Scientific studies show that by the time the average Bus Stop Mommy reaches the age of thirty, she's cut off and grown out her bangs at least 8.4 times. When you consider the rate at which hair grows, taking into accountant the change in growth patterns during pregnancy, the number of pregnancies, and the average barometric pressure during the month of May, that means it takes an average of, well, I don't know how long it takes to grow out your bangs but it's never fast enough.

The world supply of cute hair clips, headbands and duct tape is not adequate to keep our too-long formerly known as bangs out of our faces during the "I'm growing them out" phase. Even mature, well-educated and high society women have been known to crawl into bathroom corners and whine: "I'm not coming out until I can tuck it behind my ears!"

To make matters worse, there's an unwritten law that after a certain age (cough) there are fewer socially acceptable styles of hair accessories. Yesterday, I had a typical Domestic Errand Day, beginning with a parent teacher conference and ending with teaching Confirmation class. In between, I ran to the post office, Lowes, Harris Teeter, Pier One, Book Traders, Target, Blockbuster and the library. Because of the conference and an after school dental appointment, I didn't make it to the bus stop. This proved to be a fateful error.

During confirmation class, I noticed an unusually high amount of elbowing among the kids, but it wasn't until my son slid under the desk and tried to become invisible did I realize why. Barbie. Curse her, her cute figure and her stupid barrettes. Why were those hideous plastic things still in my daughter's drawer? Why didn't I have my contact lenses in before I did my hair? Why didn't anyone say anything to me?

The worst part about growing out your bangs, beyond the headband headaches and proper barrettes, is the frequency at which you'll change your mind during the process. As soon they're grown out and tucked carefree behind the ears, that first deep wrinkle or pre-menopausal zit will appear on your blatantly exposed forehead. *More* magazine will say bangs make us look younger. *Good Housekeeping* will tell us the oils in the bangs help moisturize our face and thereby diminish fine lines (which you won't see if you have bangs in the first place). Who's a girl to trust?

That's the easy part. Head to the Bus Stop and ask The Mommies. No headaches, no elbowing, no polite lies. They'll tell you the truth, then hand you a pair of scissors or a barrette. Age appropriate of course.

Other Stuff

Silly Lawsuits

Never one to be left out of the fun, I've designed my own silly lawsuit. First we had the woman who figured her thighs would make a nice cup holder for a scalding hot cup of coffee. Then came the tobacco lawsuits. In between were thousands of claimants demanding billions of dollars for irreversible, crippling, emotional trauma after suffering from a hangnail or bad dog grooming.

I'm going to consume massive quantities of Twinkies and Ho Ho's. Then I'm going to sue Hostess for billions of dollars. After all, they knew those Twinkies and Ho Ho's would make me fat, yet they continued to produce, market and sell them.

Furthermore, they produced, marketed and sold them to millions of housewives in the 1960's and '70's who in turn fed them to their children. Children like me and other poochy tummied Bus Stop Mommies across America.

Deemed the Mother of All Snacks during my childhood, I can still see the Ho Ho's and Twinkies in the kitchen cabinet. My mom added an almost sacred aura around those white boxes by keeping them separate from the other mundane snacks like raisins and pretzel rods. If I opened the corner cabinet that housed casserole dishes, mom knew I was contemplating consuming a cream filled creation typically reserved for the illustrious brown bag lunch.

Experts now know that during the formative years, children's bodies develop fat cells. These fat cells never go away, but expand or shrink according to later eating habits. Whether or not Hostess knew this fact back when they coerced my mother to buy their cellophane sealed rolls of pudge is irrelevant. This is a silly lawsuit, remember? It needn't be logical.

I will ascertain that Hostess formulated their Ho Ho and Twinkie recipes with a secret addictive agent that remained in my fat cells throughout adulthood. The agent was triggered upon the birth of my own children and reached the shopping cells in my brain the day I pack my kids' first school lunch. Now the vicious cycle will start all over again and my children will be doomed to lives of Hostess snack cake addiction. So you see, it is for them and all future generations of children that I must take action against the evil empire that is Hostess.

Flipping through an issue of *People* magazine, I learned I'm not alone in my reasoning. A girl is suing McDonalds for making her fat. I don't know about you, but in all my years of standing in line for a Happy Meal, I never once saw an employee hand out free fries or threaten a customer to "Get it Super Sized or else!"

But hey, why should she be held accountable for her own actions when she can legally peg it on someone else? Now where did I hide those Twinkies?

Rainy Day Ramblings

Maybe I need a hobby. Today I found myself lifting the lid of the wash machine to watch the clothes agitate. I saw a feather float by and counted the seconds until it resurfaced. I contemplated how badly I wanted to dive in after a pencil stub. There's something kinda creepy to me about sticking my arm way down into the bottom of a full washer. (Yes dad, I turned it off first.) It's like something might bite my fingers off and then how will I turn the clothes right side out?

One nice thing about lingering over the wash load is the heat. What is with this weather? Yesterday I had on the air conditioning and today I've cranked up the furnace. I mean, there's just something a little disconcerting about getting mentally and physically acclimated to sunscreen and bug repellent season then being forced to remember what temperature on the thermostat will activate the heat.

My friend e-mailed this morning. Her husband has the week off of work and has taken over the household chores, including her two little boys. She's going to spend this gray day working on her scrapbooks, reading and napping. Sounds heavenly to me. Except I still have this laundry to do, dinner to defrost and killer dustbunnies under every horizontal surface in this home on which I could possibly nap. The fear of them revolting and eating me in my sleep would keep me from relaxing let alone closing my eyes. My dog has no fear of dustbunnies, just cats. He's been napping all day and I'm quite envious.

I thought about making a nice big pot of chili for supper, but realized I didn't have all the ingredients. We'll eat toast for dinner before I go out to the grocery store in this weather. Even the idea of running next door to Racheal's to borrow some beans is daunting. Maybe if I call her she'll cut out a little mast from a paper plate, glue it to a straw, tape the whole thing to the beans and sail them on over.

One good thing about all this rain is that it makes me glad I didn't wash my windows or my car over the weekend. I'll have to remember the ever-possible threat of rain the next time I'm tempted to do something as silly as window washing. Perfectly good waste of a sunny day and all that stuff.

Hey look guys, it's really pouring now. Didn't anyone tell that group of concerned citizens and pastors that they could stop praying for an end to the drought? Did they go on vacation to some remote tropical island that doesn't get The Weather Channel?

I suppose I should take advantage of being stuck inside to catch up on some bill paying, closet cleaning and ironing…Then again, I think I'll go see what the spin cycle looks like.

This was the first of ten, count 'em ten, snow days that winter.

Captain's Log for Wednesday, December 4ᵗʰ

I have been informed of a strange earth custom, practiced mainly by Americans. More than an ordinary holiday, it brings to the average school child a euphoric sense of glee and liberation. I can only compare it to the earthling behavior previously observed on Christmas morning.

The parental units do not view this strange earth custom with the same joy as the children. Again, like Christmas morning, they appear weary and dreadful, as if they've stayed up all night assembling a bike and double mortgaged the house to pay for it.

The other similarity between the human celebration of Christmas Day and this newly observed strange earth custom, is the weather. It is cold; with odd shaped crystal like particles floating in the air and coating the earthen surface until even it looks pristine. It is similar in consistency to meteor ash but much tastier when caught on the tongue.

The name of this strange earth custom, Spock informs me, is, A Snow Day.

I intercepted the electronic communications of two ordinary American suburban housewives to learn more about this Snow Day phenomenon.

Subject line: HELP!

"Okay, Karen. Write about one of these days all of us moms dread... Snow Days. Of course it would be one thing if our kids could actually go outside and play in snow. It's just ice now. Mine are inside driving me crazy and making the dog wilder than usual... if that's possible. I'm already looking for the Advil and it is only 10:30. Pray for me. Amy"

"Amy, I'm making my kids work on school projects that are due next week. I'll send them to your house when they're done. Oh! Look out your window, it's starting to snow! Love, Karen"

"Karen, You're not funny. I can't tell you how many times I've yelled to the kids because I thought the roof was falling in. I have half the neighborhood kids in this house. They keep coming over. I'm sending them out into the snow now. Amy"

"Praise the Lord, Amy! I think I hear Snow Plow Man making his way into the neighborhood. There is a God."

"Dear Karen, You're hallucinating. That was the UPS truck which is nothing to get excited about since they don't wear brown shorts in this weather."

"Amy, have you seen my kids? I'm not kidding. I came out of the bathroom and found three wet gloves, one shoe, two hats, an icicle and muddy dog prints scattered across the kitchen floor. The back door is wide open and their unfinished poster boards are flapping in the breeze. How much Advil do you have left? Karen"

"Stay away from my Advil, woman! Do you take bottles away from babies too? Unless of course you have some Chardonnay you're willing to share."

"It's out on the back deck keeping chilled. But Ames, my girl, get a hold of yourself. It's only 2 O'clock."

"Listen smarty pants, you obviously haven't heard they've cancelled school again tomorrow."

"Time stands still on a Snow Day. Your place or mine?"

Flying Noses and Other Signs of Spring

My close personal friend, "Julia" from Proctor and Gamble, sent me another close and personal e-mail. Honestly, I'd feel so cut off from the outside world without her. In her latest letter, Julia gave me (and 379,000 of her other friends) tips on "stepping out into spring."

I appreciated her encouragement to get off the couch and get outdoors. I did promise myself that once it got warmer I'd walk the dog more, do yard work and breathe un-recirculated air for longer than it takes me to walk to the bus stop and back.

Ol' Jules said to get the kids off the couch and send them outdoors too. This woman is smarter than I thought. She told me to "Take a casual approach to getting your kids to watch less TV — create some outdoor action to sway them away from the screen."

Hmm, what kind of action can I create to lure them outdoors but still look casual doing it? Sirens? Naw, I don't think the police would appreciate the fake distress call. Although if this rain continues, I won't need to fake it.

During a downpour reprieve, I dragged the family out for a walk. I followed Julia's suggestions on how to "keep in touch while you keep moving." #1 "Get a family history. Ask your parents or grandparents to walk with you. Tape them as they talk about their life." This was tricky since all three grandparents live in Florida. We tried talking on cell phones while we walked, but the conversation was cut short when Grandpa Rinehart got so lost in his WWII stories that he walked into a parked car.

#2 "Play Frisbee golf. Throw Frisbees to various targets: a tree, porch steps, mailbox, and 15 other landmarks. Tally the attempts it takes to reach each target. The player with the least number of throws wins." We made this extra challenging by anointing any car exceeding the 25mph speed limit one of the 15 other landmarks. This was fun until a throw went astray and the neighbor's dog ate our Frisbee.

#3 "Go wild. Kids will get a kick out of a walk around the local zoo or wildlife preserve." We didn't have to go far out our back door for this one. I told you I needed to do yard work.

#4 "Pick your own berries or apples. Head for the farthest field for more of a workout." We met some new neighbors this way. I doubt we'll be talking to them again anytime soon.

All that walking and fleeing from angry neighbors made us hungry. Good thing Julia included suggestions for spring eating. "Grin and Grill It: Grilling is as American as apple pie. The onset of spring sends noses flying into the air as the aromas of neighborhood barbecues tempt us all. Step up to the grill and go for it."

I'm firing up the grill now. Beware of flying noses.

Goodbye Garden

The novelty of my garden has finally worn off. Over the weekend, I yanked the remaining plants and heaped them into my current, novel endeavor, the compost pile. I felt a little guilty pulling up plants that still had produce and flowers on them…but I can barely pass off fried green tomatoes to my family let alone frost bitten green tomatoes. They had a good life; it was time.

This was only the second gardening attempt of my adult life. You'd think I was the only person who ever produced a pole bean the way I celebrated my so-called success. You have to understand that I can kill a house plant, and have, by just looking at it. Forget talking to plants. I tried that once and they got up by their roots and ran away to the neighbor's kitchen. I've killed more potted herbs than the Feds.

Still very naïve about this whole gardening thing, I figured it would provide me with the quiet, meditative time missing from my daily routine. That, and put a few fresh vegetables on the dinner table for my kids to whine about.

I envisioned it being an almost spiritual experience—silently praying for friends and reflecting on the natural beauty of the Creator as I thinned seedlings, picked peppers and poisoned insects. Naturally, my children, who typically become invisible or comatose whenever the words, "I need your help." are spoken; now wanted to be super duper hands on helpers. My garden became, instead of a haven, a hotbed of activity.

They gave tours to their friends, the mailman and the meter reader. They developed a new and intense interest in soil content, the gestation period of eggplant and city watering restrictions. They picked ripe produce without being asked. They put out buckets when it rained and watered the garden without being asked. For the love of God they even pulled weeds.

One day, I was enjoying a rare quiet lunch, reading a mindless novel, when the kids came inside demanding my attention. Ever notice how they don't need you until you start to eat or pick up the phone?

Anyhow, my daughter had a colander full of lettuce and my son had shoes full of mud. "Mom, the garden's watered, fertilized and treated with Sevin dust. We tied up the tomato plants since they're growing faster now and according to Mr. Goforth from the Extension Agency, it's time to plant pumpkin seeds. Where are they?"

So much for my peaceful garden paradise…but then we did have a nice little family project going here. Do you know how rare it is to get every family member to agree on a single activity? I went out and spent $100 on kids' garden gloves, scaled down garden tools, hats, kid safe bug repellent, sunscreen and plant markers. I came home all excited to bond with my children in the sacred soil of the earth.

Suddenly it was too hot to garden. "The trick is to get out early in the morning when the air is still and the sun is low in the sky." They said summer was for sleeping in.

Besides, the bugs were really getting bad. "I bought you repellent. Use it." They said it smelled funny and made them itch.

Besides, it's hard to get the dirt out from under their fingernails. "Use the gloves I got you." They interfered with their grip, I was told.

Besides, all their friends were going to the pool…couldn't they join them there? I conceded and sent them off with the hats and sunscreen…left once again in the solitude of my garden.

Best $100 I've ever spent.

I received this and similar notes after this column ran:

Karen, I read "Has Anybody Seen My Date Book?" in the *Tampa Tribune*. It was great, and my husband agreed that you took a day out of our life as a model for your article. I gave up on my handheld Compaq because I was forever letting the battery run down, etc. Now, my date book has my life's data written in it. I have to admit that St. Anthony has come through for me a couple of times! Thanks for writing my story!

—Joan

And yes, I eventually found it.

The Lost Date Book

I have an anxiety pit stuck midway in my gut that won't go away until I find it. That book holds every orthodontic, dentist, veterinary, car, medical and school appointment for every family member for the remainder of the year.

My life as I know it is over. I might as well crawl back into bed and never come out. I lost my date book.

There are the maternally requisite recordings of every friend and family member's birthday, anniversary, vacation and flight number crammed in there. Also included are sacred, oft-dialed phone numbers and secret Bus Stop Mommy codes, that if placed in the wrong hands, could wreak suburban havoc above and beyond what any bad hair day or parent teacher conference could do.

I've ripped apart the house. It's not in the dog's bed, kids' bathroom or refrigerator. I checked the computer desk, couch cushions, crack in between the washer and dryer, cleaning supplies caddie, phone book drawer and recycling bin.

Against my better judgment, I called my husband at work. It's his fault when I can't find anything around this house, you know. I mean, if I can't get mad at him for not knowing where I left something, what's marriage for? "Where's the last place you saw it?"

"If I knew that I'd know where it is, right?" In my mind I'd a clear picture of the date book on the passenger seat of my minivan…but I wasn't going to admit that to him.

Then he said it. "Can't you just buy another one?" Sure, like I can just buy another child?

We returned last night from a 12-hour drive to Florida. If my date book were in that van, I'd have known it. A desperate woman, I crawled inside the van anyway. Under the passenger's seat I found a single mitten and my favorite winter scarf securely wrapped around the power seat gears. I flicked aside an oatmeal cream pie, bits of Chex Mix and some fingernail polish chips.

Still no date book. The search wasn't a complete waste of time though. I found an apple, still firm with skin intact, under the driver's seat. A couple more weeks of not knowing it was there and I'd have been yelling at the kids to put their shoes back on.

At my wits end I decided to do what any smart woman should. I called my mother.

"Did you pray to St. Anthony?"

"I haven't had time Mom; I've been too busy looking."

I hung up the phone, took my mother's advice and hit my knees. "Dear St. Anthony, please help me find my date book. It might not seem as important as other requests you've gotten today, like a car title or diamond ring, but it's sacred to me."

Lo and behold, the clouds parted and a booming voice came down upon the cul de sac. "Can't you just buy another one?"

Men, Dogs and Others

This is truly my mom's favorite column, but she won't admit it in front of my dad.

His Good Ideas

We took down the Christmas tree this weekend. I count it as one my least favorite tasks, so I procrastinate. Fortunately, January 12th was still the Christmas season (albeit the last day thereof) according to the Church calendar.

"Boy, that piece of wood made all the difference in the world!" It was about the third time in ten minutes my husband said it. The oft-overrated and misunderstood beast known as the tender male ego probably needed a stroking at this point; but I just couldn't do it.

I sweetly smiled, agreed and left it at that. Except I was not conditioned to just leave things "at that." I was raised to debate, cajole and justify. I was also conditioned to take credit where credit was due. Growing up, humility was not one of the principal virtues extolled around my kitchen table.

However, it's one of the key virtues of a happy marriage and I'm trying to adjust accordingly. After fifteen years, I can comfortably say that my mother was right: It's not a good idea until it's his.

Wives are the brainchild of the family. We come up with all sorts of brilliant ideas that go unheeded until they are uttered from the male mouth.

The board was my idea. A year ago. As in Christmas, 2001. After a day in Boone, we were home with our fresh cut tree—an eleven-foot excuse for instant divorce.

Perhaps it was the fresh mountain air and excitement of our first North Carolina Christmas, but it seemed like a grand idea at the time. Besides, we hadn't had to lift it yet. Or figure out how to make it stand without a root ball.

So there we were in our front yard with this eleven-foot carcass wrapped in red nylon netting. We dutifully sawed the bottom of the trunk until it fit securely in our tree stand. All four of us carried the beast inside, no one wanting to admit how heavy it was. Why ruin the festive spirit?

We stood the tree up in the family room, scraping the ceiling then and the next eight times we attempted to prop it back up. Seems our tree stand wasn't made to hold the Abominable Snowman; which is exactly what our tree looked like after we tied it to the walls and cabinets.

But before Mr. Abominable was born, Scott went to Lowes for a new tree stand. "Get a 4 by 4 piece of plywood while you're there. I think if we attach the stand to the wood it'll give the tree a wider base for weight distribution and balance." Did he listen? No.

The new stand crumpled and bent from the weight of the tree. Pine needles, sap and raw nerves flew everywhere. Muttering under my breath about plywood and attorneys, I scrounged up the hammer, nails and rope.

This Christmas, we settled for a conservative nine footer. This Christmas, we wee prepared. I bought a tree stand that specified, "holds up to a ten-foot tree." And Scott made sure the tree didn't enter the house until he laid down his newly purchased 4 x 4 board. It was his idea you know.

The Extra Child

The Extra Child. You know the one—after the third day you look him square in the eye and say, "Listen to me boy. If you're thirsty or hungry in this house you better learn to help yourself because my son, your friend, through no lack of training or nagging on my part, will not think to offer you anything. This is where we keep the glasses. Here's the pantry. The microwave is self-explanatory and I put an extra electric toothbrush head with your name on it in the bathroom drawer. Make sure you use it."

The Extra Child is over at your house so often you start treating him like your own children. No more maintaining that nice exterior for the sake of company. "All right kids, tooth brushing time. And three full minutes tonight! I know you've been slacking off. I can tell whenever I come within two feet of you. Whoever left their shoes in the middle of the doorway better move them and I mean now. Did you get sunscreen on your back? Turn around. Let me check. Who left their socks on the kitchen table, again?"

My favorite Extra Child, Carlos, is every parent's dream thirteen-year-old. I want to bow before his parents in pure reverence of their child rearing abilities. Carlos is the type of kid, unlike your own food devouring, mess creating flesh and blood, that scratches the dog's belly when no one else will, thinks the little sister is the best invention ever and always shares the Nintendo controls. He compliments and eats every morsel of food I put in front of him, speaks in complete, coherent sentences and never forgets to say Thank You.

"Hey boys, how 'bout some breakfast? Or lunch?" I asked at 11:17 this morning. My son grunted. Carlos chuckled politely for my benefit, then laid into his friend, "Morgan I've been waiting since 9a.m. for you to wake up so we could eat."

"Carlos!" I yelled across the kitchen and into the family room (the only place they'll sleep); "You need to get up and have breakfast on your own or you'll starve waiting for him to wake up. Either that or kick Morgan awake so you two can eat together. Personally, I'd opt for the second choice."

"So would I." Extra Child snickered.

"Mom! I just lost my trust in you!"

"Well son, sometimes moms have to use tough love." Even if that means ganging up against your full-time son with the part-time one.

My phone conversations with other mothers these days tend to go one of two ways: "Hello Julie? This is Karen. Can I keep your son? He fits in here so well and anyhow, the dog likes him the best. What if I trade my son for yours? I'll throw in my car...." OR "Hello Gladys? This is Karen. Karen Rinehart, your next door neighbor. I was wondering if you wanted your son back anytime soon. You know, kinda tall and lanky, blond hair, blue eyes, size 12 shoe, a star shaped birthmark on his left calf, appetite of Godzilla? Oh. Well, could you send over his underwear, socks and shot records?"

I guess I should be glad, enormous grocery bill not withstanding, that my son and his friends are still willing to be in my presence. I always aspired to be that ultra popular '70's Kool-Aid Mom....

The Life of a Loser

You'd think I'd be satisfied simply being a loser in my children's aging minds…but no, I want to be an even bigger loser. Hollywood style.

Have you heard about the goody bags that Oscar attendees receive? Businesses and designers fight and pay big for the right to provide party favors for attendees. It doesn't matter that these people already make zillions of dollars and never lose an ounce of sleep over how to pay for their kid's braces or piano lessons. If it's free, give 'em three.

Like all little girls, I had my big dreams of what I'd be or do when I grew up. One of them was to play the piano on the theme song for the Mary Tyler Moore show. Another was to be a famous actress, complete with all the glamour, five-inch stilettos and trophies. I could see myself walking the red carpet, waving to adoring fans and making the most quoted acceptance speech in Hollywood history.

"I'd like to thank the academy, my family, producer, hairdresser and most of all, Betty Crocker."

In my little girl mind, losing was not an option. Today, I'd take the stigma and disappointment in a heartbeat. This year's Oscar Loser Bag contained $7000 worth of gifts, including a pair of Vera Wang sunglasses ($150), a digital pen that remembers and organizes everything you write with it ($200), a gift certificate for Lasik surgery ($4000) and mink lined slippers.

Since so many of those actors and actresses are anti-fur, I could go home with a few extra pair for my family and friends. "Hey Meg, you're not really gong to wear those slippers after last month's protest rally are you? Can I have 'em? Thanks!"

Oh, and the gift "bag" is not the kind I buy at the Dollar Tree and stuff with tissue paper for tape-free gift wrapping. It's a $500 piece of Burberry luggage.

I'd love to be a loser at the Grammys too. This past February, participants received gifts worth $21,000. Besides the traditional "basket," celebrities "shopped" in the Gift Lounge – a room stocked with free goodies provided by vendors hoping stars will be seen in public wearing their $500 Stetson hat or $300 wireless headsets.

I wish I could've been a fly on the wall to see who took what. Did Faith Hill grab a few Mattel My Scene dolls for her daughters? I wonder which smoothie drinking stars went for the $150 Sunbeam blender? Celebrities could time the length of acceptance speeches with $525 watches and take photos with $130 digital cameras. Would they lower themselves to carry around a The Sak purse that retails for only $58? Or take the free stay at the Fairmont Miramar Hotel only worth $1500?

But what I really want to know, is who among that smiling group of capped, bonded and bleached teeth still needed the $600 gift certificate from BriteSmile. And do they want to trade it for a pair of mink lined slippers?

My husband is a creature to be pitied. That is, if you believe the sympathetic comments he gets from readers who feel I expose him raw through my candid column. So this one's for him and all the other helpful, hands-on husbands who don't view the dishwasher as an insult to their masculinity.

Doofus Dads vs. Helpful Husbands

My husband, I'm not ashamed to admit, can iron circles around me. Not only is he good at it, he'll polish off an overflowing basket in about an hour while simultaneously watching cable TV and via his cell phone, smoothing out yet another television broadcast crisis at a race track half way across the country. Two hours and back-to-back episodes of Trading Spaces later, I'd still be wrestling with the inbred crease marks on a cuffed pair of non-wrinkle khakis.

Scott can take three dishes of unidentified leftovers out the fridge and turn them into a gourmet one-dish wonder with a skillet and a stovetop. We've had neighbor kids go home and ask their dads whey they can't cook like Mr. Rinehart. What they don't realize is that there are days Mr. Rinehart would starve if he waited for Mrs. Rinehart to plan a meal.

Once upon a time I said I married Scott because he knew the answers to all the obscure but burning questions like: When will reruns end and the new television season begin? What was the name of the paymaster on the USS Eldorado during Pearl Harbor? Who carried the ball on the 3rd down and 4 of the 1983 Alabama verses Penn State game? And why is film sold at 12, 24 and 36 exposures?

Okay, truth be told, he had a better temperament than I and was tall. With me being Italian, opinionated and short, I figured he'd give our children a fighting chance for normalcy.

These days, it's incredibly handy he remembers his high school algebra and science so he can help our 13-year-old with his homework. Let me diagram a sentence to death but please don't make me read an algebraic equation.

I don't know if your husband is like mine or like the ones portrayed in current television commercials. If you're not taking advantage of the break to go to the bathroom or change out a load of laundry, you'd see the media painting American Dads as total Doofuses.

"But Karen," argued one of the Bus Stop Mommies, "They are Doofuses. They'd be helpless without us."

"Yeah, well, let's just save that for the Bus Stop…work with me here. Christmas is coming, remember? Besides, the ironing basket overflow has reached crisis proportions."

The Orange Juice commercial is one of the worst. Picture a typical chaotic school morning with three kids of all ages running in and out of the kitchen, causing cereal explosions, hanging upside down out of chairs, yelling Indian war cries, gulping down orange juice and generally creating all sorts of ruckus.

The mother, being a mother, smoothly hands out breakfasts, lunch boxes, shoes and forgotten books two beats before the kids know it's forgotten and rush back in a panic to find it. All the while, the Doofus Dad is sitting at the kitchen table, smack in the middle of the tornado-like chaos, reading the paper. After the kitchen is quiet (and the mom is undoubtedly searching for the vodka to put in her OJ) the father looks up from behind his paper and innocently drones, "Are the kids awake yet?"

Another favorite is the Kenmore Blue Commercial, the Sears brand of residential carpet cleaners. The announcer chirps, "You need the new Kenmore Blue if you have pets, kids or messy dads!" Can you just see the domestic scene with some Doofus Dad, after 40 years on earth, still unable to drink a coke without spilling it all over the family room floor? Kenmore Blue ranks dads right up there with two-year-olds and the family dog.

Then there's the Circuit City spot. The cashier is ringing up an overflowing cart of swanky electronics for a daddyish figure and says, "Some kids are going to be real happy this Christmas!" Doofus Dad looks frantic and replies, "Kids?? (nervous chuckle) I'll be back!" He runs off into the store and the next thing you see is him back at the checkout with a gazillion more items. Now the cashier says, "My wife loves this DVD." Pan to panicked Doofus Dad: "Uh, wife?" Off he runs again….

Let me tell you, if the dad in this household was that Doofus, I'd have run off a long time ago.

Father's Day

Here we go again, Father's Day. You know it's coming without the benefit of a calendar. The retailers tell you. Just like you know Mother's Day and Valentine's Day are fast approaching when the jewelry store fliers start falling out of the newspaper. It's like we're not supposed to buy jewelry the rest of the year. (Gentlemen, that was a joke. Go shopping anytime.)

According to American retailers, American Dads don't do much but play with power tools, golf and wear socks. My husband said he if hears the radio ad or sees the television spot for Home Depot one more time he's going to hurl. What are they calling themselves, Daddy's Playground? I believe my husband would enjoy getting pruning shears for Father's Day as much as I'd enjoy getting a mop for Mother's Day.

I was tilling the front yard last weekend when the thought struck me; here in the Rinehart house, things are slightly different from the smiling zombie-like "stick a bow on a drill and be happy" Father's Day commercials. After my husband helped our daughter bake biscuits, I loaded the empty gas cans in the minivan and headed to the gas station. I tilled the yard, yanked out roots, spread pine straw, shoveled, raked, wielded the chainsaw and pruned.

Taking a break, I popped my head in the back door and bellowed, "Hey, someone bring me a cold one, will ya? I'm dying out here." The waft of the air-conditioned air hit my face. I lingered long enough to notice the sweet smell of spray starch and hear the faint hisses of steam. My husband was ironing.

There I stood, covered in sweat, mud and half of what used to be my front yard, with bugs and twigs in my hair, scratches on my legs and tacky sunburn lines from my sports bra straps sticking out under my tank top.

I was the happiest woman in the world. I've said it before. I hate to iron. Give me a chainsaw, paint scraper, hammer, lawn mower and dirt under my nails. Just don't make me iron.

I called my friend Amy the other day. Her son answered, "Hang on Mrs. Rinehart...MOM! MAWMM, Can you come to the phone? (yelling even louder) I said can you come to the phone now? It's Mrs. Rinehart. Or should I tell her to call back? What?" Behind his shouting I heard a loud engine rumbling to a halt and the unmistakable hollow sound of the outdoors.

"Hello?"

"Uh, Amy, are you busy?" She started laughing, "Oh no, just out here on my John Deere. Come on over." I went outside and walked up the street. There was Amy riding around her yard, covered in grass and sweat, the dog chasing her all over.

I don't think her husband is getting a power tool this Sunday either.

My Dog Hank

Anytime I talk about my dog, I get asked the same question. "What kind of dog do you have?" Every time I give the same answer. "Stupid."

We named him after the great canine legend, Hank The Cowdog. We hoped that by osmosis or some other big word, our puppy would grow to be as brave, wise and musically inclined as his namesake. Fat chance.

He was Mighty Dog sans the cape. With a single leap he was over our fence and those of three neighbors. Except he didn't know how to reverse the path and get home. I'll never forget the day ol' Ruby came home to find my rear sticking out of her doggie door as I tried to lure Hank out of her garage with a milkbone.

In our next house we installed an invisible fence and clipped on the shocker collar. Hank saw cats. Hank chased cats. Hank got shocked, yelped and kept running. We met lots of new neighbors. I became known as "the lady with the dog that always runs away."

We upgraded to the "Stubborn Dog" collar. The shocker unit is the size of a sandwich. Hank saw cats. Hank chased cats. Hank got shocked, yelped louder and kept running. I inadvertently taught the kids next door new words. I met more neighbors. I called my husband (Hank waited to run away until Scott was traveling) and screamed, "You need to do something about this dog!" He reminded me that the kids and I conspired against him to get the dog in the first place.

One day I watched Hank bark at a cat in our backyard. There was two feet of space between them. Hank barked ferociously. The cat yawned. *Finally!* I thought. *The dog has learned his boundaries. He won't get shocked to reach the cat.*

The next day I observed Hank lounging in the exact spot the cat sat the day before. My dog is afraid of cats.

His inherent survival tendencies are much like that of our children: Good thing he's cute or else he'd be a memory. Unlike our children, we have the advantage of reminding Hank that we rescued him from the city pound death chamber. He should be grateful and act accordingly. Our children, we can only hope, will show gratitude for us giving them great genes and a pantry full of sugar bomb cereal.

Hank tested those tendencies again this weekend. When it started to rain, we called him in for the night. No Hank. I jumped in the van and the boys headed out on foot. I found him around the corner, offered him a treat and watched him run. After an hour, I decided hamsters were underrated and went home. My headlights shone in our yard onto the most innocent looking dog, curled up in his favorite spot, as if he'd never left.

Good thing he's cute.

As For The Dog Naming

My friend Alma, who swore up and down her kids weren't ready for a dog, rescued a little black fur ball off the highway. Henceforth, Midnight Destiny came to join the ranks of other Bus Stop Pets. At the risk of Midnight growing up to be a showgirl, I always add something like Immaculetta or Bernadette after "Destiny" when addressing her.

This reminds me of my brother Jimmy and his family's new dog. Huey, their faithful Golden Retriever, who'd seen them through their newlywed days and new-parent haze, took his final nap last Easter. Before the last jellybean was devoured, the campaign for a new dog began.

Their kids begged, whimpered, cried and groveled, but my brother and sister-in-law swore up and down they weren't getting another dog for quite some time. Certainly not before they fenced the yard – which would have to wait since they needed a new roof and gutters on the house which had to fit in somewhere between the badly needed new carpet and kitchen flooring.

They got the carpet, dog, but no fence. I'm so proud of my nieces and nephew for their persuasive whimpering. Looks like I did something right during their stays at my house.

It seems nothing my brother's family does is dull or ordinary. Naming their new mutt was no exception. He e-mailed me the saga:

"As for the dog naming...Janet (his wife) informed me that this is the 'kids' dog'. She, being delusional, believes that they'll assume full responsibility for feeding, grooming, potty training, discouraging embarrassing doggie habits, etc. This theory exited stage right this evening when the aforementioned canine relieved himself on the new dining room carpet and Janet sprung into action to remove the offending poopsicle.

Back to this being the kids' dog. They were given the responsibility of naming the dog. To prevent bloodshed, I was the Elections Official. Each child was sent to a separate room and asked to write down their 5 favorite dog names. I placed the names on a ballot (containing only 13 names as there was some duplication due to earlier lobbying) and asked the children to select their three favorites from the list.

The choices: Mickey, Lucky, Fido, Rover, Moby, Buddy, Buster, Shadow, Chico, Lefty, Fat Tony, Homer, and Spanky. The voting resulted in a five-way tie between Mickey, Buddy, Fat Tony, Homer, and Spanky. The five names were placed on a final ballot, and Mickey won in a tightly contested contest. The Florida results are still pending."

As I stared at the screen and thought, *good thing those kids weren't responsible for naming a child*, another e-mail appeared, this time from a dear friend. "It's official! I'm 8 weeks pregnant. The kids are already drafting lists of possible names, including Bullwinkle, Boris, or Rocky if it's a boy, and Natasha if it's a girl...."

See what I mean?

Heroes at the Bus Stop

We've heard a lot about heroes lately. I've even witnessed a few heated conversations as to what exactly constitutes a hero. Is someone a hero because they're killed doing their job? Does it make a difference if they were a librarian or a soldier?

Did the soldier need to be in active combat or simply in uniform? Is the rescuer the hero and the rescued just lucky or are they both heroes? Is one a bigger hero than the other? What's the difference between being lucky and being a hero?

I don't know or care to debate it, but I can say this: In my little Bus Stop Mommy Universe, I have a few heroes of my own.

A husband who rearranges his schedule, forgoes golf with the guys and handles the home front so his wife can run away for the weekend.

A dad who spends his Saturday helping his daughter paint her model rocket, even if it means two trips to the store to get just the right paint and stickers.

A dad, who when he has to go into the office on the weekend, takes the kids with him.

A dad who turns off the television when his son asks him to play ball, even when it's the 4th quarter, last inning, final lap or 18th hole.

A husband who knows his wife's underwear size and isn't afraid to use it.

A husband, after a frantic call from his wife, ("It's pooping on my brand new curtains!") comes home midday to get a bird out of the house. Additionally, he doesn't use it as embarrassing conversation fodder at the next social function.

A mom who's sick as a dog, but still needs to get out of bed, make lunches, get the kids to school, attend two meetings and meet a deadline.

The husband with the sick wife that says, "Go back to bed honey. I'll take care of everything." And he does.

A parent with a backbone who's not afraid to ask themselves, "Who's the adult and who's the child here?"

A parent who after threatening, "I swear young lady if you do that one more time you're grounded!" regrets it, but still follows through.

A teenager who goes against the grain and teasing from his peers to do

227

the right thing.

A friend who offers to watch your child for five days so you can go out of town with your husband.

A friend who listens to you whine and complain about your bad day and stressful problems that are ten times smaller than hers, but she's still genuinely interested and concerned for you.

A little girl who, when thrown off a horse and into the mud, gets right back in the saddle.

Every mom who starts each day praying for the grace not to scar her children for life. Then gets out of bed.

Now that's heroic.